ROSES & RODEO

Formatting and Interior Design by Bella Media Management.

First Pink Zebra Publishing Paperback Edition

13 Digit ISBN: 13: 978-1477559918

ROSES & RODEO

CHEYENNE MCCRAY

PINK ZEBRA PUBLISHING
SCOTTSDALE, ARIZONA

CHAPTER 1

"He sure is one sexy bull rider." Danica Cameron looked at her friend Kelsey then nodded toward the chute and the next cowboy preparing to ride a bull. "What's his name?"

"Darryl Thompson." Kelsey sighed and twirled a strand of her long blonde hair around her finger. "Only two dates and I think I'm in love."

"Then I hope he's Mr. Right." Danica glanced at the bull rider before moving her gaze back to her friend. "I really don't want to see you get hurt again, Kels."

Kelsey smiled. "Darryl's different than any guy I've ever dated. He's a *real* man."

Danica returned her friend's smile. She'd known Kelsey for a couple of years now and she'd grown to care for her like a sister.

They'd met at the local gym where Danica worked out three times a week and had started working out together. Eventually they began meeting outside of the health club and had become close friends.

With a smile, Danica turned her attention to the upcoming rider.

They had seats that hugged the arena, with a perfect view of all the action at the May Las Vegas professional bull riding competition. The air smelled of dust and animals and the announcer's voice carried over the loudspeakers along with medleys of tunes to go with the high-energy crowd in the arena. The intro to Lynyrd Skynyrd's *Sweet Home Alabama* blared from the speakers followed by a burst of Loverboy's *Working for the Weekend* and then a partial tune Danica didn't recognize, all in close succession.

Like other bull riders, Darryl's protective vest and his shirt-sleeves were covered with patches from various sponsors.

The announcer shouted out, "Darryl Thompson riding Killjoy, one of the rankest bulls here today."

The gate to the chute swung open and the crowd cheered as the bull flung itself out and the cowboy started his ride. The bull bucked and twisted round and round, trying to throw its rider off as cheers and shouts rose up from the crowd.

Kelsey stood and screamed, "Go, Darryl!" as he hung on for the full eight seconds and then the horn blared.

The bull bucked Darryl off before he could dismount and he landed on his hands and knees, and scrambled to his feet. The cowboy clowns—who were now called bullfighters—distracted the bull to keep it from going after its rider and they got the bull to exit the arena through an open gate that they shut behind him.

Even Danica, who didn't know a hell of a lot about bull riding, knew enough that she was sure it had been a really good ride.

Danica tilted her head to the side. "I always wondered how they get the bulls to twist in circles like that."

"Did you see that strap around the bull's flanks?" Kelsey said. "It's called a flank strap. That's what makes the bulls kick because they're trying to kick it off. The rope that the cowboy holds onto is called a bull rope."

Danica smiled as she pushed her long dark hair over her shoulder. "You're becoming quite the expert now that you're going out with Darryl."

"I'm trying." Kelsey grinned, her pretty gray eyes lit with excitement. "But I really want to be an expert on the bull rider himself."

Danica laughed. "I'll just bet you will."

Kelsey hadn't grown up on a ranch like Danica had, so to Kelsey, cowboys were a novelty. She'd met Darryl in San Diego at a country western bar and had talked Danica into flying to Las Vegas for a girl's weekend to check out the bull riding competition. Well, the bull riders for the most part.

She'd known from the beginning that this was really a girl-and-cowboy weekend. Last thing she wanted to be was a third wheel, so she'd planned to keep herself busy and let Kelsey enjoy her time with Darryl.

Danica felt her phone vibrate in the pocket of her jeans. She drew it out and saw that she had a text message from Barry.

Where are you, babe? I stopped by your place and you weren't home.

She frowned. "I'm not your babe," she muttered.

Kelsey glanced at Danica. "What did you say?"

"Got a text from Barry." Danica sighed. "He won't take a hint. Not even an outright, 'I don't want to date. Let's be friends.'"

Kelsey shook her head. "Never did understand what you saw in that spoiled little rich boy."

"He was actually pretty cool at the start." Danica pushed hair behind her ear. "He was friendly and fun. I just didn't see how obsessive he was until after we started dating. Or how arrogant and conceited he really is."

He had been the first non-cowboy she'd ever dated, and he might be the last. She rolled her eyes at that thought. That wasn't fair—not all men were like Barry.

The announcer shouted, turning her attention back to the event. "Ninety points for Darryl Thompson, making him tonight's leader."

Kelsey clapped her hands and looked at Danica. "That's a great score."

Danica nodded but looked down at her cell phone. "I'd better respond or he'll never stop sending messages."

She drafted a quick message.

In Las Vegas with Kelsey. Will be home tomorrow.

After she hit *send*, Danica raised her eyes and her gaze fixed on the next rider who was preparing to lower himself onto his bull. "Who's that?"

"Creed McBride." She gave Danica a sly smile when Danica glanced at her. "Hot, isn't he?"

"Hard to tell." But something about the cowboy made Danica sit up and take notice. There was an ease and confidence in his bearing that she could feel, even from where she sat. And yeah, when she got a good glimpse of him, he was definitely hot.

"Defending two-time World Champion, Creed McBride, ladies and gentlemen," the announcer shouted over more pulse-pounding music. "Today he's matched up with one of the toughest bulls, Dark Shadow!"

The chute seemed to explode open as the bull twisted its massive body into the arena, its rider gripping the bull rope. Danica held her breath as the eight-second ride seemed to draw out. The rider made it all look effortless as his body moved in tune with the creature's bucks and pitches.

And then the horn was blaring and the rider dismounted. He hit the ground on his side and rolled to his feet, barely missing the bull's hooves.

Danica let out her breath with relief when the cowboy avoided getting trampled. Every time a rider got bucked off or dismounted, her body tensed. Despite having four older brothers, all cowboys, she'd never been able to understand a man's need to put himself in danger like that.

"Tell you what." Danica looked at Kelsey. "I don't think I'd ever be able to date a bull rider. The sport is too dangerous."

"Lots of professions are dangerous," Kelsey said. "Police officers face danger every day."

Danica shrugged. "That's different."

Kelsey rolled her eyes. "Come on, Danica. Don't worry so much."

"You know I'm not a worrier." Danica gave a laugh. "I just

don't want to date someone who could end up hospitalized from being trampled by an animal that weighs two thousand pounds."

With a shake of her head, Kelsey said, "Hard to believe a cowgirl like you wouldn't want to date a cowboy like that."

Danica decided to change the subject. "How are the rides scored?"

"Four judges score both the bull and the rider and each judge gets a total of fifty points," Kelsey said. "Each of the judges can award up to twenty-five points for the bull and twenty-five points for the rider. They combine the points from the four judges and then divide that in half to come up with the rider's score. From what Darryl told me, no one has ever received a hundred points in the Professional Bull Riders organization. I think somewhere around ninety-six or so is the highest ever awarded."

Her phone vibrated again and she looked down at the phone.

Why didn't you tell me you were leaving? Call me when you get back.

Danica ground her teeth and tucked the phone away in her pocket again. She didn't intend to respond again and she didn't intend to call when she returned to California.

"Ninety-two point ride for Creed McBride." The announcer's voice cut through her thoughts. "That puts him over the top into first place and makes him champion!"

Danica clapped along with everyone else. Creed waved his black western hat and the crowd cheered even more.

"So you'll come tonight?" Kelsey asked when Danica turned

to her.

"If you insist." Danica smiled at her friend.

"I insist." Kelsey searched the arena with her gaze obviously looking for Darryl. "Maybe you'll get to meet Creed."

"Oh be still my heart." Danica held her hand over her heart then laughed. "I wouldn't say that is a must-do on my list."

"Just you wait." Kelsey gestured to Creed who was now talking to someone in the ring. "That looks like one cowboy worth getting to know."

* * * * *

"No thank you." Danica turned down yet another offer from a cowboy to buy her a drink.

After she declined, she dismissed the cowboy with a genuine smile. She moved away to search the room with her gaze for Kelsey. She held onto her beer bottle as she moved through the crowd.

The bar was packed with men and women in western attire and a country-western band had been playing familiar tunes all night. She liked that the slot machines were outside the bar and the constant ringing and cha-ching of machines wasn't competing with the good music.

She'd caught herself lightly tapping her boot since she'd come into the bar, but she hadn't been in the mood to dance. Usually she did, but tonight she had a headache that alcohol hadn't been able to kick. Thank goodness smoking had been banned from bars and restaurants in Las Vegas or her headache would have magnified.

Her gaze slid past Creed who had three women around him. Kelsey had called the women buckle bunnies, female groupies.

From what she'd seen, the groupies tended to wear tight jeans and boots with skimpy tops and bright, flashy accessories like a belt with a big buckle that had lots of dazzle.

She moved her gaze away from the cowboy and groupies then spotted her petite friend who was leaning against Darryl, her hand on his chest, looking into the tall cowboy's eyes. It was a sweet, romantic picture the way he was looking at her. Danica hoped Kelsey wouldn't get her heart broken. She'd been through far too much and she deserved a good guy. Danica had met him earlier in the night when Kelsey had introduced them. He seemed okay, but she'd reserve judgment for later.

Her cell phone had vibrated in her pocket three separate times. She was sure they were messages from Barry, so she didn't bother to look.

From the corner of her eye, she found herself looking at Creed. This time a woman who looked upset was talking with him and the buckle bunnies were gone. He reached up and brushed something from beneath her eye with his thumb. He said something to her and she nodded, then turned and walked in Danica's direction. The woman bumped into Danica, nearly making her drop her beer bottle.

Danica took a step back and shook her head. She looked at Darryl and Kelsey again. They really did look like a cute couple. She glanced away from the pair to check her watch. It was still early but she really wasn't in the mood to party. Maybe she'd tell Kelsey about her headache and that she was going to head up to their suite in the casino resort hotel that was on the strip. She wouldn't mind a bath in the amazing jetted tub.

"Heading off so early?" The deep drawl caught her attention.

She immediately loved the male voice and turned to find herself facing Creed McBride.

She raised her brows. "Who says I'm leaving?"

He gave a slow, sexy grin. "Honey, you've been trying to head out that door all night."

Her face warmed. "You've been watching me?"

"Ever since you walked into the room." He searched her gaze. "Just waiting for a chance to catch your attention. I don't think there's a cowboy in this place who hasn't offered to buy you a drink."

She studied his eyes. He had dark hair and nice eyes that were a gorgeous shade of green. "Who's to say I'm not going to send you packing?"

His gaze held hers. "I'm hoping my luck will hold out. I think this is the longest conversation you've had with any cowboy you've met tonight."

Amusement sparked in his eyes as he spoke. He had that same ease and confidence in his manner in person as she'd seen before he'd ridden that bull and even after his ride.

He was about as tall as her four brothers, around six-two, but a little younger—she'd guess about thirty-three. His white shirt and Wrangler jeans fit him oh-so-well, and his white western hat was tilted up enough that she could study his eyes. He was definitely hot in an alpha male, bad boy kinda way.

"I'm Creed McBride." He held out his hand.

"My name is Danica and you're right, I'm heading up to my room." She smiled as she took his hand. "Nice meeting you," she added but couldn't get herself to turn away. In fact she had a hard time getting herself to release his hand. His grip was firm and warm, his hand callused from hard work.

It was probably only seconds but it seemed as though it carried on longer before she finally drew back her hand.

"Pretty name." He looked like he wanted to touch her again to keep her from leaving but held himself back. She didn't know why she thought he did, but she could almost feel the brush of his fingers against her cheek even though he hadn't reached for her at all. He studied her and she felt warmth go through her at the intensity in her look. "I bet you're told all of the time what gorgeous blue eyes you have. Such a brilliant blue," he said.

"Is that a pick-up line?" She raised an eyebrow.

"You know it's not." He smiled. "It's an observation."

It was true that she got that all of the time. She and her four brothers had the same eye color and her aunt called them "Cameron blue".

"Are you sure you wouldn't like to two-step with me?" Creed gave a nod to the dance floor. "I haven't had a chance to dance all night."

She wanted to ask him why not when gorgeous women had surrounded him all night, or the other woman he'd been talking with, but she didn't want him to know that he'd captured her attention tonight, more than once. Fortunately, she didn't think he'd caught her at it.

Darryl came up to Creed's side and he put his arm around Creed's neck. "Do you know who you're talkin' to?" Darryl raised his beer bottle with his opposite hand. "You should be damned impressed. This is Creed McBride, two-time world bull riding champion."

Creed looked uncomfortable and Danica's lips twisted with amusement as she teased him. "I'm impressed by a lot of things, but riding an animal out to kill you isn't one of them. I'm more impressed by the person."

"Felt the heat on that one." A slight grin curved the corner of Creed's mouth, obviously knowing she was teasing, and he disengaged from Darryl. "Why don't you go find that cute little blonde you've been with all night?" he said to Darryl.

Darryl turned his gaze on Danica and slowly looked her up and down. Disgust flowed through her at the blatant way he was undressing her with his gaze. "What about this sexy thing?" He grinned. "Danica, right?"

"Yes." She folded her arms across her chest. "Best friend to Kelsey Richards. Where is she, by the way?"

Darryl jerked his thumb over his shoulder. "She's waiting for me by the bar."

Danica put her hands on her hips. "I think I might need to go have a talk with her."

"Just havin' a little fun." Darryl straightened. "I best be getting back to Kelsey."

Danica frowned, wondering if she *should* go have a talk with her friend. But then Danica wondered if maybe she was reading too much into the way he'd been looking at her.

Darryl touched the brim of his hat. "Ma'am," he said politely, his demeanor completely changed. Darryl slapped Creed on the shoulder then turned and headed toward the bar where Danica caught a glimpse of Kelsey.

"Come on." Creed indicated that dance floor with a nod. "Give this cowboy a dance."

The only indecision that warred within her was the thought of getting to know him better, maybe even liking him, when she'd already decided that she wouldn't want to date a bull rider. Not that dancing with him meant that he even wanted a relationship with her.

Against her better judgment, she found herself nodding. "All right."

He flashed a smile at her and took her by the hand. She set her beer bottle on a table as they passed by and then they were on the dance floor.

It was a lively two-step and they fell into the dance as if they'd been doing it together forever. She'd been country-western dancing since she was a little girl and it was obvious he was plenty experienced, too.

When the one dance was over, another tune started right away and he swung her into a country waltz. She found herself laughing as they danced and then she realized her headache had vanished. Every touch of his hands sent warmth throughout her body. Or was that just the heat of her skin from dancing?

She was ready to walk off the dance floor the moment the next song struck up, a slow tune, but Creed took her by the hand then brought her into his arms, catching her off guard. She braced her palms on his shoulders to keep him from holding her too close. He leaned down to whisper in her ear.

His warm breath caused a shiver to run through her as he murmured, "Thank you for the dances."

She swallowed, trying to not let his closeness affect her...the solidness of his body, his masculine scent, and the heat of his large hands at her waist. She cleared her throat but couldn't get anything out.

"I'd like to see you again," he said close to her ear.

She drew back and gave him a skeptical look. "You're a bull rider. You don't stay in one place for too long."

"Long enough," he said. "Where are you from?"

"I'm from southern Arizona, in the San Rafael Valley," she said. "But I now live in San Diego."

"There you go." He gave her a little grin. "We do have something in common. I'm from just north of Phoenix, in Kirkland, between Prescott and Wickenburg." He touched a lock of her long, dark hair. "What's an Arizona country girl doing in San Diego?"

"I work as a research associate at the University of California," she said. "In our department we do breeding maintenance, genotyping, cloning, and other related projects."

"I'm impressed." He continued to lightly play with her hair. "Did you go to the University of Arizona?"

She nodded. "Yes."

"I graduated from the U of A twelve years ago," he said with a grin. "I'd bet you were at least eight years behind me."

"Something like that." She smiled. "What was your major?"

"Animal Sciences."

The song ended, surprising her. The time had passed faster than she'd expected.

"I'd better go," she said as they drew apart.

"Why?" He walked beside her as she left the dance floor.

"It's getting late." And she was becoming far too interested in this bull rider.

He caught her by her hand and drew her to a stop. "Sure I can't talk you into a drink?"

"You already talked me into dancing with you." She smiled. "But no, not a drink."

"Give me your phone number," he said. "I want to see you again."

She shook her head. "I don't date bull riders."

With a laugh he said, "Why not?"

"It's too dangerous a sport," she said. "I'd be worried all the time."

"You'd worry about me?" He had that sexy grin again.

Somehow she felt off-balance by his reply. "I suppose I would, if we were dating. Which isn't a possibility because, like I said, I don't date bull riders."

"Why don't you give me a chance?" he said. "I'll show you that you don't have to worry about me."

She put her hands on her hips. "How many bones have you broken over the years? How many concussions have you had? How many times have you had to be stitched up?"

He winced.

"Or," she went on, "maybe you should just tell me what bones you *haven't* broken. Yet."

He shook his head. "It's not as bad as it sounds."

"Oh?" She folded her arms across her chest. "How many times have you ridden even when you were injured rather than waiting for those bones and injuries to heal?" She didn't wait for an answer. "More times than you can count, I'll bet."

He laughed and raised his hands. "Aw, come on, Danica. Just give me a chance."

She liked the way he said her name. His voice had a raw, sensual quality about it. "I'm heading up to my room now," she said. "It really was nice meeting you."

"So you're staying here," he said as she turned away and he fell into step beside her.

She realized her mistake when she'd said "up to my room." She paused mid-step and shook her head as she faced him. "Good night, Creed."

"I know when I'm not wanted." A smile was on his lips though when he said the words. "Good night, Danica."

As she walked out of the bar and made her way to the elevators, she found it hard not to look over her shoulder. She could feel him watching her and if she looked, she might find herself turning around and going back.

CHAPTER 2

It was early morning and Danica rubbed her bleary eyes with her thumb and forefinger as she entered the sitting room of their suite, her bare feet padding over the soft carpet. She glanced at the door to Kelsey's room and saw that it was open. Was Kelsey up?

She went to her friend's room and peeked in. The bed was made, Kelsey's clothes still scattered over the foot of it. She was a disaster when it came to cleaning and keeping her belongings in order.

Danica frowned. She hoped Kelsey was with Darryl and safe. Kelsey had a history of picking the wrong men and Danica sure hoped that Darryl wasn't one of them.

The doorknob to the suite rattled and then the locks clicked as Danica turned to face the door. Kelsey stepped inside and closed the door behind her. She looked tired and rumpled in the same jeans and blouse she'd worn last night, but she also looked happy.

Relieved to see her friend, Danica went to Kelsey and took her by the shoulders. "I take it you had a good night."

"A *very* good night." Kelsey grinned and hugged Danica. She smelled of both her familiar orange blossom scent and a more musky, masculine scent. When Kelsey drew away she was still smiling. "I think Darryl could be *the one*."

Danica raised an eyebrow. "Where have I heard that before?"

"This time it's for real." Kelsey sobered a little. "He's not like the others."

Danica didn't want to rain on Kelsey's parade, so she brightened her tone. "So I take it you got lucky last night?"

"Did I ever." The look of a satisfied woman was on Kelsey's face. "That man doesn't just know how to ride a bull."

Danica forced a smile. "Sounds like a match made in heaven." More like the man had taken advantage of a woman who had an infatuation with him. Hell they barely knew each other. She kept those thoughts to herself as she studied her friend.

"Mmmhmmm." Kelsey made a dreamy sound and looked up at the ceiling. She returned her gaze to Danica and she gave a mischievous grin. "Saw you dancing with Creed McBride last night. How did things turn out with him?"

"They didn't." Danica pushed her hand through her hair and gave a tired smile. "I told him I wasn't interested in dating a bull rider. Told him I'm impressed by a lot of things, but riding an animal out to kill him wasn't one of them."

Kelsey clapped her hand over her mouth then moved her hand away. "You didn't."

"Of course I did." Danica shrugged. "I told you how I feel about it."

Kelsey shook her head. "I can't believe you said that."

Danica had to laugh at the expression on Kelsey's face. "I told him that before we danced so I think he took it well enough—I'm sure he knew I was teasing. He still wanted my number."

"I take it you didn't give it to him." Kelsey looked disappointed.

"Nope," Danica said. "Said goodnight and headed straight up here."

"You're crazy." Kelsey laughed then moved toward her bedroom. She stopped in the doorway with her hand on the doorframe, looking over her shoulder at Danica. "I could always give your number to Darryl who could give it to Creed—"

"No." Danica folded her arms across her chest. "Uh-uh."

"If you're sure," Kelsey said.

"I'm positive." Danica pointed her finger at Kelsey. "Don't you dare."

"You're no fun." Kelsey laughed then turned away and moved into her room. "Maybe I will, maybe I won't…"

"Kelsey…" Danica said in a warning tone.

Her grin still mischievous, Kelsey closed the bedroom door behind her leaving Danica shaking her head.

* * * * *

Getting through the line at the security checkpoint at the airport felt like it took forever. Everyone and their mother seemed to be leaving Las Vegas at the same time. After going through security, Danica put her shoes back on, returned her laptop to her backpack, picked up her duffel bag, and headed to the gate where she would catch the plane back to San Diego. Kelsey was staying a couple of extra days to spend more time with Darryl.

In some ways Danica wished she would be flying into Tucson then driving home to the San Rafael Valley. As much as she enjoyed living in San Diego, she had to admit she was homesick. She missed her brothers and her young niece. She'd traded wide-open spaces for a large city on the ocean and even though she enjoyed her job, she wasn't sure sometimes that she'd made the right decision.

She settled herself into one of the plastic chairs in the waiting area and put her backpack between her feet and her duffel beside her. She started to dig through the backpack to find her e-book reader when a male voice captured her attention.

"I must be the luckiest man in Vegas."

Her gaze shot up and she met Creed's gaze. Pleasant warmth traveled throughout her. "Oh. Hi."

He gestured to the empty chair beside her. "Mind if I join you? I've got about an hour before my flight takes off."

Butterflies tickled her belly and she immediately had to reprimand herself for feeling a little excited about talking with the tall, hot cowboy again. "Sure." She gave a casual shrug.

He settled into the seat and relaxed in a casual male pose. He had a worn black duffel at his feet and wore brown boots that were clean but clearly broken in. His Wranglers were faded and fit him well and he wore a plain black T-shirt along with a straw western hat on his dark hair that was pushed up slightly and she could get a better look at his gorgeous green eyes.

He was even more handsome up close and personal in the

daylight where she could clearly see his tanned skin and the smile lines around his mouth. He was clean-shaven and he had a spicy, masculine scent. His eyes glittered with interest as he studied her in return.

"Headed back to San Diego?" he asked in the soft drawl that Arizona cowboys tended to have.

"I have to work Monday." She rubbed her palms on her jeans. "Off to the next competition?"

"Not yet." He shook his head. "Need to stop home and check in with my mom." The corner of his mouth curved into a smile of fondness. "Haven't been home for a while and she worries."

"I wonder why," Danica said dryly.

He laughed. "There are worse things than dating a bull rider."

"You mentioned last night that your family's in Kirkland." Danica adjusted herself in her chair so that she could talk with him better as she changed the subject. "I imagine they're ranchers."

"McBrides were some of the earliest ranchers to settle in that part of the state," he said with a nod. "Sometime back in the eighteen hundreds."

"Sounds like we both have deep roots. It was the same for my family in southern Arizona." Danica pushed her long hair over her shoulder. "Camerons were among the first to arrive."

"San Rafael Valley?" he asked. "Around Sonoita and Patagonia?"

She nodded. "About twenty-five minutes outside of Patagonia."

"There's a competition over Labor Day weekend in Sonoita," he said. "I was thinking about heading there."

She raised an eyebrow. "Little old Sonoita is big enough for pro bull riding?"

"It's become popular and has been attracting crowds from all over central and southern Arizona." He rested his ankle on his knee. "It was added to the circuit just this year and it will be televised."

"Wow." She shook her head. "Have I ever been out of touch with my home area. In two years things seem to have changed."

"I'd like you to come to the competition." His words were filled with a certain conviction that reminded her of her four older brothers. She'd never met a man who quite measured up to them.

She shook her head, but said, "Maybe."

He gave a sexy little grin, as if knowing he had her. "Rather than waiting that long, there's a competition in Prescott coming up soon."

"Whoa." She held up her hands. "I'm not going to be following you from competition to competition like one of your groupies. As a matter-of-fact I don't plan on seeing you ever again."

"What can it hurt, Danica?" The way he said her name made her feel a little gooey inside.

"We've been through that." She put her palms on her thighs. "I'm not going to date you, Creed. So give it up."

"I'm no quitter," he said in a teasing tone, but his eyes were serious.

Her phone rang, thankfully breaking the train of conversation they were on. She glanced at the caller ID then looked at Creed. "Just a moment. I need to take this."

She answered as she held the phone to her ear. It was her doctor's office calling with the results from her well-woman visit. Then she was transferred into the nurse's voice mail instead of to the nurse herself, and was instructed to leave a message with her phone number. She identified herself then rattled off her number before disconnecting and tucking the phone into the outside pocket of her backpack.

When she looked at Creed she found him studying her. "You're tough," he said.

"So I've been told." She smiled. "That's what growing up with four older brothers will do to a girl."

"We've got that in common," he said. "I've got four older brothers myself. Wouldn't that be some family reunion?"

She found herself picturing her now very large family with her brothers, four sisters-in-law, and her niece, and then Creed with his four brothers and who knew how many were married. And then she wanted to slap herself upside the head just for letting the thoughts enter her mind.

They fell into a conversation about what it was like growing up the youngest of five. From a couple of the stories they each told, it sounded like Creed's brothers were a lot tougher on him than Danica's brothers were on her.

"Even though they teased me and played pranks on me, to tell the truth, they spoiled me." She crossed her legs at her knees. "I got away with a lot growing up. They would even take the blame for some of the things I pulled, just so I wouldn't get into trouble."

"I'd like to meet them sometime," Creed said.

An announcement came over the loudspeakers loud enough to interrupt their conversation. It was the call to board the plane to San Diego.

"That's me." She got to her feet and Creed stood.

"I want to call you." He took her hand and squeezed it.

"Like you said, you're no quitter." She didn't withdraw from him immediately. "But I'm stubborn as hell."

He laughed. "I can see that you are."

She drew her hand from his. "Take care, Creed."

He touched the brim of his hat. "I'll be seeing you, Danica."

She shook her head but returned his smile then turned and joined the line of people ready to get on the plane.

As she stood behind other passengers, she felt Creed watching her and couldn't help looking over her shoulder at him. With his hands tucked into his rear pockets, he gave her a nod but she couldn't read his expression. He looked so good standing there and she had a sudden feeling, like déjà vu...like they'd done this before.

The feeling made a shiver shoot down her spine and she turned away, determined to not look back at him again. She took a deep breath as the line started to move forward at a faster pace.

Why hadn't she just given him her number? What would it hurt to talk to him again? She sighed. Maybe she was being too stubborn. But then again, maybe not.

She still felt his gaze on her as she entered the ramp and headed down to the plane. It was almost a relief when she knew he couldn't see her any longer.

It was time to put one ultra-sexy cowboy completely out of her mind and get back to her life.

CHAPTER 3

It was always good to get home after a trip. Danica blew out a breath as she let her backpack slip from her shoulder and onto the couch in her living room and tossed the duffel beside it. Even after nearly two years her townhouse didn't have the same warmth and hominess as the home she'd grown up in on the ranch. She'd surrounded herself with pictures of family and touches of home with western décor, but of course it wasn't the same.

Sometimes she felt lonely even though she'd had plenty of friends and no shortage of men who wanted to date her. But she was used to a rowdy home with four males and Aunt Grace who had raised the five of them when their parents died.

Danica kicked off her shoes then stretched out her arms toward the ceiling and did a few other stretching exercises before starting toward her kitchen for a bottle of water and lunch.

Her phone rang inside her backpack so she turned back and dug the phone out of the outside pocket. She checked the caller ID and saw that it was an Arizona area code but didn't recognize the number. She answered it with a "Hello."

"Hey, Danica." Creed's voice sent a thrill through her belly.

"How did you get my number?" she asked with surprise. "Did Kelsey give it to you?"

"I overheard you when you were on the phone," he said. "I have a good memory for numbers."

"I should just hang up," she said, but a smile touched her lips.

"But you won't." His voice held a confidence that might have irked her if it had been someone else. For some reason his self-assurance did just the opposite. It attracted her in a way that surprised her.

"How was your trip?" he asked before she could respond.

"Crowded. Full flight." She walked into the kitchen the phone pressed to her ear. "Other than that it was fine. How was yours?"

"Let's see…" He sounded like he was counting things off on his fingers as he spoke in his low drawl. "First there was the year-old twins with their mother in the seats beside me and the poor kids had twin ear infections and let everyone know about it. Then there was the woman's five-year-old son sitting behind me kicking my seat and singing "I'm sexy and I know it," while his two older brothers fought the entire trip. All in all it just reminded me of my brothers and me when we were young."

The way he said it in an amused tone made the parts about the kids behind him sound comical and she found herself laughing. "I have to say your trip was far more eventful than mine."

"Are you home?" he asked.

"Just walked through the door about five minutes ago." She headed into the kitchen and grabbed a bottled water out of the fridge. She held the phone between her shoulder and her ear as she cracked open the bottle then held the phone in her hand again. "I'm ready for a little relaxation but I have laundry to take care of and the house needs a good cleaning."

"Just managed to get out of Sky Harbor," he said, "I'm headed north now. Or I'm trying to. This Phoenix traffic sucks sometimes."

"It does." She took a long drink of water then set it on the countertop. She wandered out of the kitchen and plopped onto the couch beside her backpack that contained her laptop, causing it to bounce and almost fall onto the floor. She caught it before it fell and pushed it back to safety. "When's the next competition?"

"So you are interested." Satisfaction was in his voice.

"Just being polite," she said but smiled.

"Since you asked, the next one I'm headed to is in Montana next weekend," he said. "Then in two weeks the Cowboy Capital competition in Prescott, my stomping grounds." He paused. "I can send you tickets to the Prescott event."

"You really think I'm going to hop on a plane to go see you get beat up by a bull?"

"Yeah." His voice was low and sexy and her belly flip-flopped. "I'd like you to be there."

She put her feet up on the coffee table and wiggled her toes. "I'll think about it."

"What's your email address?" he asked.

She thought a moment. She liked talking with him, liked the way he made her feel. "If I give it to you," she said, "it doesn't mean

I'm saying yes to dating you or going to Prescott."

"You bet," he said but she heard a touch of triumph.

She took a deep breath then gave him her email address.

"Got it." There was a grin in his voice. "I have a great memory for numbers and this one I won't be forgetting."

She almost groaned as she thought about what she was doing. She was letting Creed in. But if she was honest with herself, she liked it. She liked talking with him, had enjoyed being around him.

They stayed on the phone while he drove to his family's ranch. He was easy to talk with and somehow she ended up talking with him the entire two hours it took him to get from Phoenix to Kirkland. Spending that time with him on the phone made her feel as if she'd known him far longer than less than twenty-four hours.

"Pullin' up to my folks place," he said. "I enjoyed talking with you, Danica."

"I kinda did, too." She realized her ear was sore from talking so long and shifted the phone to the other side. "That still doesn't mean I'm going to Prescott."

He laughed. "We'll see."

When she disconnected the call she shook her head. When Kelsey found out about this she definitely would not hear the end of it.

Something genuine and nice about Creed drew Danica and she knew she was about to get herself in trouble. Not only was he a man who faced danger for fun, but he also was on the circuit and on the road all of the time.

"Not a good recipe for a relationship," she said aloud and shook her head but she was still smiling when she set to work cleaning her townhouse.

She was just about finished cleaning when her phone rang again. She dug it out of her pocket and looked at the caller ID screen. *Barry Hobbes.*

With a mental groan she connected the call. "Hi, Barry."

"Hi, babe."

A flash of irritation went through her. *I'm not your babe.* "What's up?" she asked.

He sounded put out as he said, "Why didn't you respond to my last text messages?"

"My phone died and I forgot the charger. I wasn't able to get a charge until I got home." Okay, so it was a lie, but a good one. "What's going on?"

"I have two tickets to join Ambassador Baxter in his box at the ballet Friday night," he said. "I'd like you to go."

When she'd first started dating Barry, she hadn't really paid much attention to how he threw around names of those he considered important and influential, and flaunted his connections, but it had become increasingly annoying.

"Sorry." She mentally ran through excuses. Bathing a cat would be more fun than going with Barry to the ballet. "I've got something going on Friday night. In fact, the whole weekend is packed."

"What do you have going on?" he asked in a tone that told her he didn't believe her.

Clip my toenails, floss my teeth, and clean the toilets, any number of things that would be more exciting than spending time with you.

"A big project for work is going to take some overtime." Stretching the truth was better than spending another minute with

Barry since he couldn't seem to take a hint. She added, "Missing a couple of days at work has put me behind."

"What were you doing in Las Vegas this weekend?" he asked, sounding perturbed.

With a sigh, Danica said, "I went to a bull riding event with Kelsey."

"Why the hell would you want to go to a rodeo?" He sounded condescending as he spoke and she wondered why she had ever thought he was a great guy. "I thought you left all that behind when you moved here."

Danica frowned. "No, I didn't, Barry. I may be in a large city, but I'll always be a country girl at heart." She pushed her hand through her hair. "Got to go." She glanced into the kitchen at the cold stove. "My dinner is almost finished."

"I'll give you a call this weekend," he said. "We can do something next week." He made it sound that it was a foregone conclusion that she would go out with him.

She gritted her teeth then took a deep breath before saying, "Goodbye, Barry."

In an irritated tone he said goodbye and disconnected the call.

This time she did groan aloud. She'd told him not long ago that she wanted to be friends and that was it, but he kept calling. In Barry's privileged life, he wasn't accustomed to rejection and he wouldn't leave her alone until she got it through his thick skull that she wasn't interested in him anymore.

Well, he was going to have to get used to her saying "no." She broke up with him once. It looked like she'd have to sit down and have another talk with him sometime soon and do it again. She didn't want to deal with that right now and she needed to do it in person.

She went toward the kitchen to prepare dinner. Her thoughts turned back to Creed and she found herself smiling again, which was utterly crazy. She wasn't going to date the man.

But then, instead of going to the kitchen, she found herself stopping then digging her laptop out of her backpack and booting it up. Once she had connected to the Internet, she went to Google and typed in *Creed McBride*. Immediately a screen came up with the first page entirely filled with links to information about him. The top link was to his personal website.

She clicked on the link, which greeted her with a photograph of Creed on the back of a bull. Creed gripped the bull rope while holding his free hand up as the bull kicked high with its rear legs. Creed's masculine grace and the ferocity of the bull were captured in the snapshot that was a fraction of a second in the life of a bull rider.

The links included a page of upcoming competitions he would be going to; his biography; and a page filled with photographs. She perused his bio and learned about the rodeo championships he had won as a teenager, his experience, and the type of training he undertook that prepared him for his career in bull riding.

His bio referenced his idol, seven-time world champion, Ty Murray, one of the greatest champions, if not the greatest, known to the sport of bull riding. Creed had studied Ty's career and emulated him as he grew up. Creed credited his idol with being the inspiration for his success.

The article mentioned some of his injuries that had either sidelined him or he had pushed past and continued to excel. Broken ribs, punctured lung, broken jaw... She winced as she read what she believed was not a full list of his injuries and she shook her head.

She clicked on the photographs link and looked over the pictures of Creed riding bulls, and accepting awards.

After she perused his website, she pulled up links to other sites and frowned as she saw him in photographs with different women and read an article in *People* magazine about the hottest cowboys and those who were considered to be the biggest womanizers, cowboys who liked to play the field, and she frowned. Creed was high on the list of cowboys who love 'em and leave 'em.

"So Creed is a womanizer." She frowned. "Not my kind of man."

She closed the lid to her laptop feeling somehow disheartened. Why should she feel that way when she hadn't planned on seeing him again?

With a sigh of frustration, she set her laptop on the coffee table and headed toward the kitchen to fix get herself something to eat and shove aside any thoughts of Creed McBride that might try to creep back in.

CHAPTER 4

A rainbow of color shimmered on the wall from the refracted light that shone through a crystal figurine of a stallion sitting on an end table. Danica had collected horse figurines since she was a little girl and she had likenesses of horses in porcelain, wood, glass, and crystal. Most of them had been gifts.

She held her glass of wine as she stared at the rainbow that was starting to fade as the sun slowly moved in the sky and the light didn't hit the crystal in the same way. She settled on her couch, set her wine glass on an end table, and opened her laptop.

It had been a long but productive day at work and she was tired, but she wanted to check her email. Yesterday's conversation with Creed and her subsequent research weighed on her mind and she tried to push it away. Why it had disappointed her so much to read that he was a womanizer, she wasn't sure.

Several emails greeted her including two SPAM messages, an email from her brother Zane's wife, Jessie, and another from the youngest brother, Dillon, along with a note from Kelsey. And then her gaze rested on an email address that wasn't familiar but she knew who it was at once: cowboybullrider99@gmail.com.

Creed.

She closed her eyes for a moment against the sudden excitement that filled her belly. She should just delete the mail without even reading it.

Instead, she opened her eyes and clicked on the email. When she opened it she saw that there was an attachment along with a note from Creed.

Danica,

I enjoyed our conversation at the airport and on the phone. I hope you'll consider going to the Prescott bull riding event coming up. I've attached a ticket to this email. I'd sure like to see you again and show you around my hometown.

Creed

Danica sighed. Just getting an email from him made her heart flutter and something to stir inside her. She shook her head to try to shake off the feelings, but it wasn't easy. She was attracted to a man who'd left a trail of broken hearts behind him, as if the bulls he rode had stomped on them.

Odd thoughts crossed her mind. Would her brothers approve of Creed? They just about ran off every boy she'd ever dated while she was growing up, and most of the men she'd dated as an adult didn't stick around long. It wasn't easy being the sister of four older and very overprotective brothers.

What she needed was a real man who wouldn't be intimidated by the four big men. Hell, she wouldn't settle for less.

Could Creed be that man?

She groaned and thought about banging her head against her keyboard.

Her phone rang and vibrated in her pocket. She dug it out and looked at the caller ID and her pulse beat a little faster when she saw that it was Creed.

"Speak of the devil," she murmured as she stared at the screen. She could send him straight to voice mail… "Chicken," she muttered to herself then pressed the ON button and brought the phone to her ear.

She took a deep breath. "Hi, Creed."

His voice was low with a husky quality to it. "Hey there."

"I got your email." She put a positive note in her words. "Thank you for the ticket."

"You're coming," he said, his tone filled with certainty.

"I didn't say that." Her hair slid over her shoulders as she shook her head. "I just said thank you."

"I want to see you again." He had such a command to his words that it made her shiver.

"I'm not into womanizers, Creed." She didn't want to mess around with either one of their hearts.

"Who says I'm a womanizer?" He sounded almost amused.

"*People* magazine for starters."

"You can't believe everything you read." He laughed. "So you've been looking me up on the internet."

The fact that he know knew she'd been interested enough in him to do some research made her cheeks warm a little. "You can't tell me there's not some truth in what the magazine reported."

"I'll be honest with you, Danica." His tone became more serious. "I've dated a lot of women but I wouldn't call myself a womanizer. I don't go out on a woman I'm dating. I just haven't found the right woman to settle down with. I want to spend the rest of my life with a woman who fits me. A woman who's my other half. So far I haven't come close to finding her."

"I guess that's fair enough." She twirled a lock of hair around her finger. "You actually sound like a romantic."

"You could say at heart I am." He still sounded serious. "I never set out to hurt anyone. I figure you can't find the right woman if you don't look hard enough."

"So you're telling me that you don't date women for just a good time?"

He gave a soft laugh. "I've dated women who want an equally good time, women who make it clear that's all they're looking for. Is there a crime in that?"

"I suppose not." She'd done the same thing. She'd dated men for fun, and she'd left a few broken hearts behind herself.

"Then say you'll come to Prescott in August." He lowered his tone. "I want you to be there."

"I'll think about it." She sank back into the cushions on her couch and crossed her legs at her ankles. "But no promises."

"I'll take what I can get," he said. "Maybes are yesses in

disguise."

She tilted her head back on the couch. "So what's a no?"

He gave a low laugh. "A no is a yes in the making."

She smiled. "They should call you Cowboy Casanova."

"Nah," he said. "That would mean I play the field, or go out on a woman I'm dating, and that's as far from the truth as you can get."

"Okay, okay." She shook her head but still laughed. "I'll give you the benefit of the doubt when it comes to the womanizer thing. This time. Gossip magazines do tend to stretch the truth at times."

"Glad you're seeing it my way," he said then added, "The event I'm riding in next weekend is being televised if you'd like to watch."

"Are you kidding me?" She gave a huff. "It's bad enough seeing cowboys getting trampled right in front of you live. Watching close-ups of it isn't my idea of fun."

"If you change your mind it's on the sports network Saturday evening," he said. Danica heard a young woman's voice in the background but not what she was saying. "I've got to go." He suddenly sounded distracted. "I'll call you soon, Danica."

She found she was disappointed that their conversation was ending and mentally rolled her eyes at herself. "All right," she said.

His voice softened. "Have a good night."

"You, too," she said before he disconnected the call.

She looked up at the ceiling. What was she getting herself into?

* * * * *

Danica paced her living room and chewed her fingernail then looked once again at the text message from Creed on her phone.

Wish you could be here tonight. I'll be thinking of you.

She shook her head. It had been a week since she'd first met Creed and he was about to ride a bull on national TV. He wanted her to watch and she was actually considering it.

Okay, this was silly. She stopped pacing and grabbed the remote control off of the coffee table and clicked on the TV. She changed the channel to the sports network and saw that the bull riding event was just getting started.

She sat on the edge of the couch, remote control in hand as she listened to the announcers and saw the first cowboy settling in to ride. It was a matchup of the fifteen best bulls and fifteen best bull riders.

The announcers talked about the bulls and how these were scored as the toughest, rankest animals in the sport.

As the announcers turned their attention to the rider and the bull he was on, they named the rider and the bull and talked about the match-up.

The camera stayed on the first rider as he tightened the bull rope then secured his riding hand.

Other cowboys stood on the bars of the chute, giving advice and helping the rider get ready. The rider gave a signal and then another cowboy on the other side of the gate yanked the gate open.

The bull shot out of the chute and bucked three times before it tossed the cowboy off. The cowboy scrambled out of the way of the hooves, picked up his western hat that had flown off, and dusted it off on his chaps as the bullfighters worked the bull toward the exit chute.

She realized she had been gripping the remote control hard enough that her fingers hurt and she forced herself to set the remote on the coffee table as the channel went to commercial.

When they returned from commercial, Danica watched other cowboys ride bulls and get bucked off before the eight-second mark. Every time the rider ended up on the ground she tensed up even more as the bull's hooves pounded the hard earth close to the cowboy.

Darryl Thompson was the first rider to stay on his bull the full eight seconds. The announcers talked about how great Darryl's skill was and how he was hot on the tail of Creed McBride for the number one position.

Danica wondered if Kelsey was watching, too. She hadn't talked with her friend since earlier in the week. Kelsey still sounded hopelessly enamored with Darryl. Danica had checked him out on the Internet, too, and when she'd looked up images there were plenty with Darryl and any number of buckle bunnies. Danica had wanted to talk with Kelsey about it, but wasn't sure if she was overreacting. Just because she'd seen pictures of him with various women didn't mean he was a player and would hurt Kelsey. Those women were "before", like the women in Creed's past.

Right?

Her phone rang and she glanced at it to see that it was Barry. She'd managed to dodge him all week. She sent the call to voice mail and then looked at the TV again.

Another commercial break, two more riders, and then a familiar figure was in the chute.

"Creed McBride," an announcer said. "A legend in the making. He's riding Destroyer and it's the first time these two have been matched up. Not many cowboys get past two seconds on Destroyer. We'll see how McBride handles him."

"McBride is a real pro. I'd never bet against him," the other announcer said.

Danica started chewing her nail again as she watched Creed in the chute on the back of the bull. The bull thrashed around in the chute and Creed had to adjust himself and continue his preparation.

He gave a nod and the gate was jerked open and the bull shot out of the chute and into the ring.

"Look at the way McBride handles Destroyer," the first announcer shouted.

Danica wanted to cover her eyes but made herself watch every brutal second. She was amazed at how at ease Creed looked in the saddle of a beast that would kill him if he had half a chance.

At eight seconds the buzzer went off and the crowd cheered. The announcers talked in excited voices.

Creed dismounted, landing on his feet, and had to dodge the bull that immediately charged him. The cowboy clowns—or rather bullfighters as Kelsey had told her they were called now—had to work to get the bull's attention off of Creed.

When a score of ninety-three was announced, Creed pumped his fist in the air then took his hat off and waved it at the crowd. He looked directly into the camera and winked.

Danica felt like that wink was meant for her, like he knew she was watching even though she'd told him she wasn't going to. She shook her head. He was probably winking to swooning cowgirls all over the nation.

She picked up the remote and turned off the TV—she'd had enough bull riding for today, and enough of a certain cowboy that she was thinking about far too much these days.

A knock sounded at the door, startling her. She wasn't expecting anyone and she wondered who it was. She went to the door and peeked out the peephole.

Barry.

Darn it.

He knocked again and she undid the chain lock and the bolt lock and opened the door. "What are you doing here?" she asked.

"You haven't been answering your phone." He stepped past her and into her home and she faced him as she closed the door behind him. "I'd like to take you out tonight."

"I've got too much going on." She gestured to her laptop that was sitting on an end table. "I've been working." If you could call watching a bull riding event on TV working.

Barry was a good-looking man. An inch taller than her, he had light brown hair and light brown eyes. He had nice features and a great build, but he didn't seem as attractive to her as he had when she'd first met him at a beach party with Kelsey.

"You need some time off." He gave her a smile. "You can change and I'll take you out to that exclusive new restaurant downtown and then we'll go to the theatre."

She took a deep breath. "Barry, I told you I just want to be friends."

It was like he hadn't heard her as he said, "You have about thirty minutes to get ready."

She settled her hands at her hips. "I'm not going. I told you I have work to do."

He frowned. "Are you seeing someone else?"

For a moment she paused. "Yes." *Sort of.*

His expression darkened a little. "And you didn't say anything to me? Who is he?"

"That doesn't matter." She found herself curling a strand of her long hair around her finger then made herself stop. "As far as you and I, just friends, like I've told you before."

"You're making a mistake, Danica." Barry's frown deepened. "You and I—we've got a good thing together."

"We don't have anything. We're just friends." She gave an exasperated sigh. "Now I've got work to do."

He looked like he was going to say something else then shut his mouth. He reached for the front door and held the knob for a moment. "We'll talk about this later," he said as he looked at her.

She folded her arms across her chest. "Bye, Barry."

He gave a nod, opened the door, walked through the doorway, and shut the door hard behind him.

Danica groaned and leaned with her back to the door and banged her head against the wood. Getting rid of Barry was turning out to be even harder than she'd thought it would be.

CHAPTER 5

Danica hitched her backpack up on her shoulder and gripped her duffel tight as she walked up the ramp from the plane and into Sky Harbor Airport. Part of her couldn't believe she was here, but for the most part she had to admit she was excited to see Creed.

They'd talked on the phone every day for the past two weeks and had emailed each other and sent text messages. She felt like a teenager again with a crush on the cute guy in school.

When she walked off the ramp and into the terminal, she slid her phone out of her pocket and dialed his phone number. He said he'd be waiting at the cell phone lot for her plane to arrive. Apparently the cell phone lot was where people could park while waiting for someone's flight to arrive and it was time to pick them up.

"Hi, Danica," Creed said when he answered.

"I'm here." She smiled as she gripped the phone. "Where do I meet you?"

He told her which door to go to on the north curb and what kind of truck he was driving. She disconnected the call and headed for the pick-up and drop-off area of the airport, and for the first time she felt tingles of nervousness in her belly. She hadn't seen him since the airport in Las Vegas and at that time she hadn't planned on seeing him again.

When she stepped out of the building, a blast of heat hit her full in the face. She wasn't used to Phoenix heat, especially after being in San Diego, and she felt a sheen of perspiration on her shoulders and arms that were bared by her white and red striped tank top. She wore a pair of royal blue shorts and red sandals, and her hair was pulled back in a ponytail.

A red truck pulled up to the curb. She couldn't help a smile when she saw Creed behind the wheel.

The moment the truck was parked, he got out of the vehicle and she caught her breath. He was even more rugged, more handsome than she remembered. He wore a white western shirt, dark blue Wranglers, and a brown belt with a silver buckle and brown boots.

He smiled and came around to where she stood. He took the backpack and duffel from her. He looked at her like he wanted to kiss her but knew it was far too soon for that. Instead, he gave her a quick hug.

After he set her things behind the passenger seat, he helped her into the truck.

"Come on." He smiled and closed the door behind her after she'd slipped into the seat. One thing about most of the cowboys she'd grown up with was that they were gentlemen. She'd missed that in San Diego.

He strode to the driver's side and climbed in then pulled the truck away from the curb and entered airport traffic. He glanced at her. "It's damned good to have you here, Danica."

"I'm glad I came." Her lips still tingled as she studied his profile as he looked back to the road. "What's first?"

"Hungry?" he asked as he guided the truck out of the airport and she realized it was after lunch.

"Yes." One thing she'd never had a problem with was her appetite.

"I know a good Mexican place that I like to go to when I'm in this area," he said. "A real hole-in-the-wall, but damned good food."

She nodded. "Hole-in-the-wall sounds excellent."

Spending so much time talking with him over the past couple of weeks made it feel natural talking with him. They picked up where they'd left off in the conversation they'd had yesterday afternoon about classes they'd both taken at the U of A and professors he'd had who were still around when she attended.

The city view sped by as they talked and he asked her about work yesterday. Over the short course of the time she'd known him, he'd expressed a great deal of interest in her career, always asking questions and inputting his own thoughts. He was especially interested in the work she did with genotyping and cloning.

"Do you miss the country and living on a ranch?" he asked as they pulled off the freeway.

"Yes." She didn't even hesitate. "I miss it a lot."

He looked thoughtful. "Have you ever thought of moving

back to the country?"

"I have." She pushed a strand of hair from her eyes. "I enjoy my career but I miss country life and ranching, and of course family." She smiled. "Maybe one day I'll make the change. For now I'll stay put because I really love what I do."

She studied his profile. "What about you? Do you get tired of traveling and want to just go home and ranch and sleep in your own bed?"

"Yep." He glanced at her. "But like you, I love what I do."

She shook her head. "I still don't get men and the need to put your lives in danger."

He gave her a little grin. "Chicks dig it."

A laugh bubbled up inside her as she thought about the popular song he'd just quoted from. "If you say so."

He winked and pulled the car into a Mexican restaurant parking lot. Gravel crunched beneath the tires as he drove through the lot and parked.

She opened her door but in the next moment he was around and helping her out of the truck. Yes, she'd definitely missed cowboy gentlemen in San Diego.

He touched the base of her spine as they walked up to the restaurant's front door. Heat spread from his fingers, through her shirt to her skin.

Warm scents of freshly made tortillas, refried beans, melted cheese, and other delicious smells flowed over her the moment they walked through the front door. It was late for lunch so the place wasn't crowded. They were seated within moments in a booth with wooden bench seats and the server left them with simple one-page laminated menus in their hands.

"Smells wonderful in here," Danica said as her stomach growled its agreement.

He skimmed the menu. "What are you going to have?"

"Cheese enchiladas." She set her menu down almost immediately. "That's my favorite Mexican dish and what sounds good right now. And a glass of *horchata* would be great." The rice, cinnamon, and vanilla drink was one of her favorites when she could find it. Not all Mexican restaurants carried it.

"Beef chimichanga for me." He placed his menu on top of hers.

Her phone vibrated in her pocket, but she ignored it. Probably Barry sending her another text message.

The server returned and took their orders, leaving them alone once more.

"So how many bones have you broken?" She hadn't asked him those questions since the first night they met when she hadn't waited for an answer.

He studied her. "Do you really want to know?"

She hesitated. "Sure."

He leaned back in his seat. "I haven't broken anything in my left leg."

"I'm not so sure I want to see you ride this weekend." She shook her head. "I'm crazy for being here."

The server arrived with Creed's beer and her *horchata*. Danica touched her glass but didn't drink as she looked at him.

"Hey." He took her hand and squeezed it. "I'm a pro. This is what I do for a living and I enjoy it."

She nodded as she looked at their joined hands and his scarred up knuckles. She brought her gaze to his. "Two thousand pounds of fury out to kill you isn't my idea of fun."

"Just watch." He gave her a grin. "Soon you'll be addicted to it. You won't be able to help yourself."

"Ha," she said but couldn't help smiling back at him.

In moments their food arrived. One thing about little places like this one was that they tended to be fast.

Creed changed the subject and soon they were laughing and talking like they usually did. He had a great sense of humor and he could make her laugh, which was something she really liked about him.

When they finished, he insisted on paying. It was part of that cowboy code—most didn't let women pay for meals when they went out. In San Diego she'd insisted on paying half when she dated men, but she knew better than to insist with a cowboy. Maybe it was a little antiquated, but it was something she'd grown up with.

It wasn't long before they hit the road and were traveling along the I-17 Highway toward Prescott. The areas they drove through were isolated once they left the metro Phoenix area. It was a part of the state she'd only been through once and it had been when she was younger.

"Prescott lays claim to the world's first and oldest rodeo that started back in 1888," Creed said. "The professional bull riding event has been going on since 2005."

He explained how professional businessmen and merchants had gotten together and organized a "cowboy tournament" with cash prizes a hundred and twenty-five years ago. Now Prescott sponsored year-round rodeo events. He continued telling her about Prescott Frontier Days and other interesting things about the town.

Just as she was digesting all he told her, he said, "Tonight you'll get to meet some of my family." She shot a look at him and he grinned. "They're gonna love you."

CHAPTER 6

The August summer afternoon was sunny and bright as they walked toward the Old Courthouse. Even though it was hot, the temperature was considerably lower in Prescott than Phoenix. She was bound to have a darker tan by the time she returned to San Diego.

Tomorrow, Saturday, would be the bull riding event and it was a one-day, rather than a two or three-day, event. That left them some time to spend in Prescott where she had booked a bed-and-breakfast for the weekend. She didn't plan on sleeping with Creed this weekend, so she wasn't taking any chances by staying with him. She was far too attracted to the man.

Their shoulders brushed as they walked down the tree-shaded walkway that led to the Old Courthouse. Plenty of people recognized Creed and greeted him while smiling and nodding at Danica.

In more rural or less populated areas of the state, strangers met each other's eyes and gave nods in greeting, and Prescott was no different. Not everyone was polite in the old-fashioned country way, but most were.

When driving in rural areas, people raised their hand in greeting to anyone coming the opposite way as they drove past. It was another world and another thing she missed.

Birds chirped in the trees they passed under and a light breeze rustled tree leaves.

"It's a pretty town," Danica said and smiled at Creed.

"I never appreciated it until I started riding pro and was on the road all of the time," he said.

"One of those things you take for granted 'til you don't have it anymore." She nodded. "I know what you mean."

After they passed another couple who greeted them with nods, Danica asked Creed, "Are you going to retire here someday?"

"Yep." He smiled. "I plan to buy a ranch and work it somewhere between here and Wickenburg."

"Creed!" A female voice came from behind them and both Creed and Danica turned.

A beautiful slender and petite blonde in her mid-twenties, about Danica's age, rushed up to Creed. Her braless breasts bounced beneath a skimpy top with spaghetti straps and her jean shorts were rolled up high enough that her butt cheeks probably showed from behind.

Danica frowned inwardly. She'd seen that woman somewhere before. And then she realized it was the same woman who had been with Creed at the bar in Las Vegas, and she'd been crying.

The young woman threw her arms around Creed's neck and she started crying again.

"I need to talk to you," the blonde said with a sob.

Creed glanced down at Danica. "Give me a sec," he said then walked away with his arm around the woman's shoulders.

When they were a fair distance from her and she couldn't have heard the conversation if she tried. Before she turned away, she glimpsed the blonde's tear-stained face and red eyes.

Not much longer and Creed returned. He looked troubled.

"Everything all right?" she asked.

"It will be fine." His phone rang, and he drew it from his holster and answered it. "Hi, Mom." He was silent as he listened. "Yep, I'll be there at seven Sunday night."

When he'd holstered his phone he smiled at Danica. "Let's go to Courthouse Plaza."

"You lead, I'll follow," she said.

He offered her a smile and she returned it.

She couldn't help but wonder who he'd been talking with but decided if he didn't volunteer the information it was none of her business.

They strolled around Courthouse Plaza then spent time in historic downtown Prescott including Whiskey Row, which was being rebuilt after having gone up in flames not that long ago.

As the day wound down, they went to a great barbeque place in Prescott where Danica had a shredded pork sandwich and Creed had the baby back ribs. They had cowboy beans, coleslaw, cornbread, and ice-cold beer to go along with it.

When they walked out of the restaurant, Danica covered up a

yawn. It had been a long and relaxing day.

"You're not tired yet, are you?" He put his arm around her shoulders. It felt comfortable and…nice.

She had to tilt her head to meet his eyes. "A little. I was up late last night finishing up a project for work so that I could take today off."

"Why don't we go ahead and get you checked in to that bed and breakfast," he said as he guided her in the direction the truck was parked.

She nodded. "Good idea."

It didn't take long to drive to the small, quaint two-story inn. Danica signed in with the motherly woman who was at the front desk and paid for her room with a credit card. She was given an old-fashioned key to a room at the patio guesthouse and was told that she had the Cleome room.

They walked the short distance to the guesthouse. Creed took the key from her and opened the front door. Her room was down the short hall and he used the key to open the door to her room.

It was so pretty and quaint that she fell in love with it at once. A burgundy, green, and cream quilt covered the king-sized bed along with mounds of pillows. There was a rocking chair, an over-stuffed chair in front of a fireplace, and a flat screen TV. On one end was a small kitchenette along with a bistro table and chairs.

In the bathroom there was a huge jetted tub and a marble shower, which looked oh-so-tantalizing right now.

Creed set her things on the rocking chair then moved to where she stood. When he was just inches from her he reached out and caught her hand. The simple touch felt intimate and it sent a thrill straight through her belly.

"Would it be taking advantage of you to kiss you?" he said quietly. "I've been wanting to from the first time I saw you."

She tilted her head so that she could meet his gaze. "You can kiss me."

He lowered his head and his lips brushed hers. It was a whisper touch that had her parting her lips on a sigh. He pressed his mouth firmly to hers and slipped his tongue between her lips.

His kiss was slow and filled with heat. It grew more intense as he kissed her and a deep, primal need grew inside her. Their kiss deepened and she found herself sliding her arms around his neck, rising up on her toes, and kissing him even harder.

A groan rose up inside him and he grasped her by her waist and pulled her tight to him. His erection dug into her belly and she caught her breath as she realized that if she didn't stop now, there might be no turning back.

She moved her hands to his chest and pushed, just enough to break the kiss. "I think this might be headed in a direction that I'm not ready to go."

He gave a pained smile. "I think you're right. If I keep kissing you like this we're both going to end up with our clothes off, trying out that king-sized bed over there."

Her cheeks warmed as she pictured the two of them on the bed, naked and sweaty, their limbs tangled together and their bodies fused as one.

She didn't want him to leave even though she wasn't ready for sex with him. "We could play cards," she said. "I'm pretty good at poker."

He gave a slow grin. "Honey, they only kind of poker I want to play with you right now is strip poker."

She tilted her head to the side. "That would be fun… Think you could keep your hands to yourself if?" she teased.

"Not a chance in hell," he said. "If those clothes of yours start coming off, they're all gonna be off in a hurry."

"Then I guess poker is out." She glanced at the fridge. "Too bad we don't have any beer or I'd offer you one."

He looked serious and she wondered why. He took her by the shoulders. "Danica, being around you right now isn't the easiest thing I've ever done. It might be the hardest." His lips firmed. "You're driving me crazy. You look great, you smell so good, you tasted incredible, and you felt amazing in my arms. I just want to touch you and I don't think I can keep my hands off you."

She swallowed. She felt the same way. He was so sexy with his afternoon stubble and the depth of the green of his eyes. She loved the scent of a man and she had loved the feel of being in his strong arms.

But she didn't tell him that, although he could probably see it in her eyes. They still didn't know each other well enough to tumble into bed already. She needed time.

"All right." She offered him a soft smile. "I'll let you go."

He shook his head as if saying no but he still said, "I'll meet you here in the morning and join you for breakfast."

She nodded. "That will be nice."

He gave her a long, lingering look before he turned and headed for the door. He glanced over his shoulder one last time, then closed the door behind him.

CHAPTER 7

Summer sun beat down on Danica as she sat in the middle of the packed outdoor arena. No breeze stirred the still air and a droplet of sweat rolled between her breasts. Before each ride, the announcers shouted out the name of the bull and cowboy about to ride it.

The crowd cheered and then seemed to hold its collective breath as another bull flung itself into the ring, a cowboy on its back. The bull bucked fast and hard, twisting its body around. The cowboy lost his grip before the eight-second horn sounded and he tumbled off the beast.

Danica gripped the wooden bleacher seat she was sitting on, her hands to either side of her as she watched the bull continue to buck and almost trample the cowboy. The bullfighters finally caught the bull's attention and got it out of the ring.

As the bull thundered down a chute, Danica lessened her grip on the seat. Every single bull ride she found herself tensing up and praying that the cowboy wouldn't get hurt. Somehow seeing it in person was far more difficult to watch than on TV. Maybe because this felt more real.

"Crazy," she said to herself, not for the first time, as the next cowboy prepared to ride. "Some men are just plain crazy."

She studied the cowboy and realized it was Darryl Thompson, who Kelsey still had a thing for. Danica had spoken with Kelsey a couple of days ago and she said that Darryl had flown out to be with her in between events. She sounded happy and excited and Danica was glad her friend had found someone she cared for. At the same time a familiar nagging at the back of her mind was worried that Kelsey would get hurt again.

Kelsey had nearly squealed with excitement to hear that Danica was going to Prescott to see Creed ride. Danica admitted that that she'd watched him on TV and that she and Creed had still been talking daily. Kelsey had wanted to make it to the Prescott event to see Darryl, but had a friend's wedding to go to.

Danica watched Darryl as he settled onto the bull. She couldn't see what he was doing from where she was sitting, but she imagined he was securing the bull rope around his hand like she'd seen on TV.

Moments later the gate to the chute opened and the bull shot into the arena. Even with a furious bull beneath him, Darryl's ride was smooth and professional and he matched the movements of the bull. When the eight-second horn sounded he dismounted, landing on his feet. The crowd cheered and Darryl took off his hat and flung it into the ring with triumph, something she'd seen a lot of cowboys do during the two events she'd gone to and the one on TV.

Darryl picked up his hat. He received a score of ninety-three and raised his hat to the cheers of the crowd. Grinning, he exited the arena.

Three more bull riders entered the ring, two of them hanging on for the full eight seconds while the third landed on the ground with the first buck.

For some reason, the bull riders' vests with patches from all of their sponsors on them made the cowboy look even sexier. She wasn't sure why their protective vests looked so good on them. Maybe it was like any man in uniform.

She rubbed her palms on her jeans in a nervous movement as she waited for Creed's turn. She had dressed as she always did when she went home or to country-western events. She wore Wranglers, a western-style blouse, and a pair of boots. Her hair was pulled back in a ponytail and she wore a western hat.

Before she knew it, Creed was in the chute, preparing for his ride. He looked focused, intent on what he was about to do.

Danica's heart pounded faster and she clenched her hands into fists as she waited for him and the bull he was about to ride, Black Rain, to enter the ring. It seemed to take forever and then it was too soon.

The bull came out twisting and turning the moment the gate was opened. The fringe on Creed's chaps fluttered in the air as the bull raged.

Creed moved on the back of the bull as if his body had been created of smooth flowing liquid. He matched every buck, every twist, and he made it look effortless. Danica held her breath for the full eight seconds that he rode Black Rain.

When the horn sounded, he dismounted, hit the ground, and rolled away from the bull. He got up and dusted himself off.

Danica let out her breath in a huff. She shook her head as the crowd cheered and shouted. Then Creed looked directly at her, touched the brim of his hat, and flashed her a grin before turning away. She felt a fluttering sensation in her belly and smiled at the grin that had been just for her.

The announcer shouted that Creed had just scored a ninety-four-point ride, beating Darryl by a point.

When the event was over, Danica was grateful. Three bull riders had been stepped on and suffered minor injuries. To a one they got to their feet, dusted themselves off, and made it out the ring on their own. One thing about these cowboys—they were a tough lot.

After she made it through the crowd leaving the arena, she headed across the parking lot and waited for Creed by his truck.

She leaned up against the truck and watched people coming to the parking lot and climbing into their vehicles. She spotted Darryl and almost called out to him when she saw that he was with someone. He had his arm around the shoulder of a gorgeous black-haired woman and she had her arm around his waist. They walked a little too close together and were a little too familiar as far as Danica was concerned.

She frowned. If Darryl hadn't broken things off with Kelsey, then he had no business being with another woman. She watched the pair until they reached a big truck and they both climbed in. Again, maybe she was reading too much into things.

When Creed came walking toward her, carrying his equipment, she studied him. He looked so damned sexy in his dusty jeans and shirt, his handsome face streaked with dirt. His eyes held the spark of a man who had just faced a giant and won. And she considered a bull quite the giant.

She didn't realize she was smiling until he reached her. "Congratulations, Mr. Champion."

He set his equipment down and then grinned as he caught her by her waist, swung her around, and set her down on her feet.

This time he didn't ask—he brought her to him and kissed her hard. Passion filled his kiss and she wrapped her arms around his neck and kissed him back.

"I need to shower." He stepped away from her and brushed a smudge from her cheek. "I'm getting you dirty."

"Why don't you come to the B & B and shower in my room?" She trailed her fingers along his jaw, feeling his rough stubble beneath her fingertips. "Then we can go out to eat like you promised, and then to the dance."

"Works for me." He kissed her again before stepping back, but caught her hand. "Sure you're okay with that? Me showering at your place?"

"As long as you don't attack me," she teased.

"I'm more concerned that you'll attack me," he said with a straight face and then laughed.

She shook her head, trying not to smile. "Let's go."

He helped her into the truck then tossed his gear in the back. When he made it to the driver's side, he took off his hat and set it on the center console as he climbed in. He started the truck and headed toward the B & B.

She looked at Creed while he drove and found desire stirring inside her. Somehow she'd gotten caught up in the excitement and it was making her want him even more than she had before. She had to admit that he'd intrigued her from the beginning. The more that she had talked with him and was around him, the more that she wanted him. And damn but he'd looked so hot riding that bull.

Maybe it hadn't been such a good idea to invite him to shower in her room.

She swallowed down the words that would tell him she'd had a change of heart. She could handle this. She could do this and not lose her head.

When they reached the B & B, he removed a green duffel bag that had been tucked behind the front seat and slung it over his shoulder. They walked side-by-side to her room and she caught his musky scent of dirt, the bull, and his own male scent that she found indescribably delicious.

For once they were quiet, which wasn't normal between them. Usually they never had a shortage of conversation. Tension filled the air between them and she knew it was a sexual tension that he felt as much as she did. It made her heart beat faster and more butterflies looped around in her belly.

No, it was not a good idea to be leading him where there was a nice, comfy bed that she really wanted to try out with him.

She bit her lip at the thought. Damn but she had to get her mind going in a different direction.

He opened the door with the old-fashioned key and held it open for her before walking into the room and shutting the door behind them. She turned and faced him and tried for a neutral expression, but was afraid her eyes gave her away.

She caught her breath when he reached up and brushed a strand of hair away from her face.

"I know I already told you once, but I can't help but say it again." His words were soft as he studied her. "You have the most amazing blue eyes. Now I know what it means to get lost in someone's eyes because I could lose myself in yours."

She looked down then looked back at him again. "Maybe you'd better take that shower."

He gave a slow, single nod. "I think you might be right."

A sigh escaped her as she watched him turn and head to the bathroom with his duffel still over his shoulder. He paused and took off his western hat and set it on the rocking chair.

He didn't close the bathroom door behind him and she couldn't take her eyes off of him as he stripped out of his red western shirt. He didn't look at her, as if he wasn't aware that she was watching.

She bit the inside of her lip as she looked at his muscular yet lean body. He had a cowboy's build and she wanted to run her fingers over his taut abs to his pecs, her fingers skimming through the light sprinkling of hair on his chest. His hips were narrow and he had a tight ass that looked so good in the Wrangler jeans that he still wore.

But not for much longer. He tossed the shirt aside and she saw several scars on his torso, no doubt from bull riding.

He reached for his silver and gold belt buckle and unfastened it before unbuttoning his jeans. She knew she should turn away but she couldn't make herself. He dropped his jeans and he was left in a pair of blue boxer briefs, a prominent bulge outlined by the material.

His gaze met hers as he stripped off the underwear. He looked hungry…hungry for her.

Heat rose to her cheeks as she saw his thick erection. She wanted to touch it, taste it, feel it inside her.

He didn't move toward her and she wondered if she should be relieved or disappointed. Instead he gave her a slow, sexy grin before opening the shower door and reaching in to turn on the water. His cock jutted out as he held out his hand and tested the water and she could barely hold herself back. He looked at her one more time before stepping beneath the spray and closing the shower door behind him.

Her face still burning, she paced away and took a deep breath. Then she paced back to the bathroom, and then away again.

Oh, this was crazy. It was absolutely nuts. She should grab her purse and leave and go for a long walk outside. And maybe when she came back, he would be dressed and she wouldn't be on the verge of jumping him.

Because that was exactly what was going to happen if she didn't leave right this very minute.

CHAPTER 8

Danica stared at her purse, her back to the bathroom. *Pick it up and leave. Tell Creed you're going to the store, going for a walk,* anything *but staying here.*

The water shut off and she went still. She couldn't move. She heard the shower door open and several more moments went by with her still incapable of movement.

She sensed him behind her, his presence powerful, and she slowly turned to face him. He stood in the bathroom doorway, a towel loose around his hips as he studied her. His dark hair was damp, the muscles in his biceps so hard and tense that his veins stood out.

He crooked his finger in a "come here" motion.

She swallowed, indecision warring inside her, but then she

found herself inches from him. She didn't remember walking toward him but now they were both standing in the doorway of the bathroom.

He raised his hands and took off her western hat that she'd forgotten she was wearing, and he tossed it onto his own hat that was on the rocking chair. He pulled off the hairband that held her locks in a ponytail and let her hair fall around her face. She shivered as he ran his fingers through the strands and lightly massaged her scalp.

With an intent expression, he brought his hands to her shoulders and the strength in them felt like they might bruise her skin.

A few drops of water beaded on his chest and she wanted to lick them off. She tilted her head to look into his gaze and saw dark fire in his green eyes. Still gripping her shoulders, he lowered his head until his lips were a fraction above hers. Her heart pounded faster as she breathed in the scent of soap and felt the heat of his body so close to her own.

And then his mouth was on hers. He kissed her with rough passion. His tongue slid between her lips and she tasted his warm male flavor and felt the wildness in his exploration.

She lost her breath as he jerked her close to him. His body was hard against hers and she felt the rigid press of his erection.

A thrill shot through her, from her belly straight between her thighs. She imagined him inside her, taking her. His kiss deepened, filled with a primal need that she wasn't sure she could tame if she tried.

She placed her palms on his chest and felt the light sprinkling of hair and the taut, smooth skin beneath her fingertips. He raised his head, drawing away from the kiss. His chest rose and fell beneath her hands, his breathing heavy, and then she realized she was breathing hard, too.

With his gaze still fixed on hers, he moved his fingers to the column of her throat to the V of her blouse and skimmed his knuckles over her soft flesh. His fingers found the top button and he slowly undid each one as he looked into her eyes.

He was waiting for her to stop him, giving her the chance to say no before it went too far. But she didn't want to say no—she wanted him far too much. Maybe it was crazy when she'd only known him a short time. Most of that time had included long daily conversations on the phone. But maybe that was why she felt so comfortable with him...and it felt so right being with him.

But was it right? What about the reports of him being a womanizer? Maybe they weren't true, but maybe they were. Did she want to be next in his long line of conquests and then be tossed aside?

What about the crying woman from the bar in Las Vegas, and then by the courthouse in Prescott? Was she another one of Creed's past conquests? Did he have some kind of relationship with her now?

And the truth was, she did barely know him.

She brought her hand up and put it over his, stopping him, as she met his gaze. "I'm sorry, Creed." She stared into his eyes that searched her own. "I—I think maybe this is a mistake. I'm letting my desire for you cloud my judgment."

She lowered her head, looking away from him. He caught her by the chin and raised her head back up to meet his gaze. "The last thing I want you to do is regret any time we spend together, Danica. I want you to have only good thoughts when you think of us."

"Thank you," she said.

He gave her a soft smile as he started re-buttoning her blouse. "Not saying it's easy, but I understand and I only want what's right for you. And what's right for you is what's right for both of us."

"I think I need to take a shower now." She stepped back. "But the bathroom door is going to be closed and locked this time."

He gave a low laugh. "That is definitely the smart thing to do."

She gave him a quick kiss then sat on the edge of the bed to take off her boots.

"Let me." He grasped her boot by the heel and tugged it off and set it aside, then did the same with her other boot.

"Thank you." She smiled at him then peeled off her socks and carried them to the bag she was using for her dirty clothes.

She went to the wardrobe where she'd hung up a few things that she'd brought with her in her duffel bag. This morning, before the bull riding event, she'd ironed the dress she'd picked out. It was a pretty royal blue eyelet western dress, the blue a compliment to the blue of her eyes. She avoided Creed's gaze as he watched her select black panties with a matching black bra and take them into the bathroom with her.

It wasn't that she didn't trust Creed… She didn't trust herself. So she locked the door behind her to avoid temptation for either of them. The tiled floor was cool beneath her feet as she started to take off her blouse. She could almost feel the brush of Creed's knuckles as she unbuttoned her blouse and her heart rate picked up.

She swallowed and tried to turn her thoughts away from what she and Creed had almost done.

"Thank God for keeping my head on straight." She sighed as she looked in the mirror. "You just about made a big mistake, Danica."

She unbuckled her belt and slipped it out of the belt loops before stripping out of her jeans and then her panties and bra and going to the shower.

As she turned on the water and let it run until it was warm, she tried not to think about Creed, naked, beneath the same showerhead that she was about to step under. She was tempted to bang her head against the shower's tiled wall but it wouldn't do her any good to get headache. Or would it?

She rolled her eyes and stepped under the spray to take a nice, long, warm shower.

* * * * *

Danica's long dark hair fell in waves over her shoulders as she walked with Creed into the dancehall and her western dress swirled around her legs and the top of her boots. He touched her elbow as he escorted her inside. They'd just had dinner at a great steakhouse and she was full.

Large wood-bladed fans hung from the open-beamed ceiling, stirring the air, and it smelled like fresh paint and sawdust. The interior walls had been painted a glossy brick red and the floor was concrete with sawdust scattered over it.

Loud country-western music filled the place and the dance floor was packed. Creed took Danica by the hand and shouldered his way through the crowd surrounding the dance floor. She wasn't sure exactly where they were going, but she liked the way her hand felt in his large one. She was a tall woman at five-eight but he made her feel petite.

Men and women greeted him, men slapping him on the back and congratulating him on his successes. Several buckle bunnies stopped him to get his attention then saw that he was holding Danica's hand and left when he didn't respond to their flirting.

"Am I cramping your style?" Danica said after the third woman left, probably looking for another bull rider to flirt with.

"What?" He raised an eyebrow.

She gestured toward the retreating back of the woman who'd just left. "You seem to be in high demand tonight by everyone."

"I told you, Danica," he said in a patient tone. "When I'm with someone I don't flirt or go out with other women. That's not my style."

"I believe you." She smiled and he squeezed her hand.

From the time they'd had that conversation about reports saying he was a womanizer, she'd found that she really did believe him. There was something genuine and honest about Creed that was incredibly attractive.

When they reached the opposite side of the dancehall, he walked up to an equally tall man who had dark hair and a hard look to his tanned face. He wasn't what she'd call good-looking like Creed was, but there was something about the man who exuded power and virility.

"Danica, this is my oldest brother, Blake." Creed turned to his brother. "Blake, this is Danica."

Blake held out his hand. "A pleasure," he said with a nod and took her hand. His grip was firm, his hand callused from hard work.

"Nice to meet you." Danica smiled as he released her hand.

"Are you here with Sally?" Creed asked.

A dark look crossed Blake's features and he squeezed the empty paper cup he was holding, squashing it completely. "No," was all he said and Danica had a strong feeling that Blake didn't want to talk about Sally whatsoever. Had the woman broken his heart?

Apparently Creed had the same impression because he changed the subject. "Have you seen Tate, Ryan, or Gage?"

Blake gave a nod toward his left. "Gage is that direction," he said in a slow drawl. "Haven't seen Ryan or Tate."

Creed clapped his brother on the shoulder. "I'm going to take Danica to meet the rest of the family."

Danica smiled and said, "It was nice meeting you."

Blake gave a nod. "Likewise."

Creed squeezed her hand and led her through the crowd. "Blake's not big on conversation," he said.

"I had that impression," she said.

They were stopped three times by people Creed knew including two bull riders and the women they were with.

Danica knew at once when they'd reached another one of the brothers because of his resemblance to Creed.

Creed introduced his brother, Gage, to Danica and they shook hands. Gage had a powerful build, dark hair, green eyes, and a sexy grin that would be enough to make a girl's heart flutter. If Danica wasn't with Creed, she might have found Gage intriguing in a different way than she did tonight.

A cute little bouncy brunette walked up to Gage. She reminded Danica a lot of a high school cheerleader, but the brunette had to be in her thirties.

"This is Chloe," Gage said as the petite woman stood next to him. He introduced Creed and Danica.

"Hi." Chloe gave a winning smile and slid her hand into the crook of Gage's arm. She turned her face up to look at Gage. "Let's dance."

Gage nodded to Danica then Creed as Chloe tugged on his arm. Gage gave Chloe a sexy grin and they headed out to the dance floor. The cowboy was quite the lady-killer.

Creed led Danica out to the dance floor and brought her into his arms. It was a slow song, and he held her close.

"Gage and Blake couldn't be more different," Danica said as they danced.

"Wait 'til you meet Ryan and Tate." He gave a low laugh. "One thing about us McBrides—no one can say we're boring."

"Yeah, I'd say that's the last thing you are." She leaned back a little, her arms looped around his neck. He wore a black shirt and a black Stetson and he'd never looked better.

Okay, maybe naked would qualify as looking better. It was hard to compare his naked, muscular form to all that luscious skin being covered up.

She mentally rolled her eyes at herself.

"You look amazing." Creed ran his thumb along her jawline and she shivered from his touch. "You're so beautiful."

She glanced away and looked at the other dancers then returned her gaze to his. "Thank you."

He trailed his fingers to her ear in a slow, erotic motion and she felt desire stir inside her. Desire that she wanted to quench, but she couldn't. It was too soon. She hadn't known him long enough.

She swallowed. "Don't."

"Don't touch you?" he murmured.

"Not like that." It was hard to get the words out. "It's too… intimate."

"I can't help but want to touch you." He studied her eyes. "You're so soft and warm in my arms."

She bit the inside of her lip before she said, "Then maybe I shouldn't be in your arms."

He shook his head. "There's no getting away from us, Danica."

She frowned. "Just because I came out to see you ride doesn't mean there's an us."

He gave her a grin that made butterflies swoop in her belly. "You're not foolin' me, sweetheart."

She tilted her head. "You've got quite the ego, Creed McBride."

"Just stating the truth." He whirled her around on the dance floor as the song concluded then brought her close to him and they fell immediately into the next song, a country waltz.

He was great at country-western dancing and she loved dancing with him. They went from the waltz to a two-step.

They left the floor when a line dance started. He hooked her around the waist with his arm as they watched and she didn't move away from him. She liked the feel of being in his embrace.

She closed her eyes for a moment. *Danica, you've got to stop this.*

But she didn't want to stop it.

Perspiration from dancing cooled on her skin as she relaxed with his arm around her and watched the people line dancing. She hadn't line danced since she left for San Diego and she found herself tapping her toe to the sound of the music.

A familiar face caught her eye—Darryl was on the opposite side of the dance floor. And the woman she'd seen him with earlier was in his arms.

Danica's whole body went tense and she gripped her hands into fists.

"What's wrong?" Creed put his hand on her shoulder and when she looked up at him he had a concerned expression.

"Darryl is with another woman and he's still dating my best friend, Kelsey." Her words were tense as she looked from Creed to the place where Darryl and the woman had been standing, but they weren't there anymore.

When she looked back at Creed he was frowning. "To be honest, your friend would be better off with someone else. Darryl isn't a good guy."

Danica returned his frown. "What do you mean?"

Creed dragged his free hand down his face. "I do know that Darryl was arrested for domestic violence several years ago. He was never charged because his ex-wife never pressed charges. Rumor is he's rough with the women, but that I don't know for a fact."

Danica's skin went cold. "I need to tell Kelsey right away. I swear if he touches her, I'll kill him."

"Morning will be fine for that," Creed said. "It's late and Darryl isn't going anywhere."

She nodded, realizing that he was right. It could wait 'til tomorrow. But first thing in the morning, she was calling Kelsey.

Creed grasped Danica by her shoulders. "You and Kelsey both need to stay away from Darryl. He's dangerous."

She nodded and he kissed her on the forehead.

"There's Ryan and Tate." Creed took Danica by the hand and

smiled at her. "They'll love meeting you."

He led her through the crowd to a pair of handsome cowboys who were standing just behind the crowd at the edge of the dance floor. When Creed and Danica reached his brothers, Creed made the introductions.

"What in the hell are you doing with a bull rider?" Ryan asked with a teasing glint in his eyes. "A bull rider isn't worthy of a woman like you."

Creed lightly punched Ryan in the shoulder then looked at Danica. "Don't listen to him. He's just jealous 'cause I have the prettiest woman in the place here with me."

"You're right about that." Ryan winked at Danica.

She laughed. It was easy to see that he had the kind of teasing nature that would be fun to be around.

Tate just shook his head, an amused look on his features. He was quieter that the others—not distant like Blake had seemed to be, but the type of man who stayed a little more to himself.

By the end of the night, Danica was tired and ready for bed. Creed took her back to the B & B and walked with her to the door of her room. He took the key from her and opened the door. Light spilled out when the door swung open.

"I'd invite you in," she said, "but I don't think that's a good idea."

He shook his head. "No, it's not a good idea. I just can't keep my hands off of you." He reached out and touched the side of her face. "What about a goodnight kiss?"

"Yes." She moved her mouth to his and when their lips met it was like flames exploded inside her. She grasped his collar and pulled him closer as they kissed each other with fire and passion that made her head spin.

He pressed her up against the doorframe, his hands at her waist and his chest hard against her breasts. His kiss was searing, sending heat straight through her from her scalp to her toes.

When he drew away from the kiss she was breathing hard. She was so close to telling him to stay when he said, "Good night, Danica." He brushed his lips over hers one more time then turned and walked away and into the night.

CHAPTER 9

When she arrived home from Arizona, Danica tossed her bags on the bed and immediately stripped out of her clothing and got into the shower. She closed her eyes as she stood beneath the warm spray, thinking about Creed.

She had sent a text message to him as soon as her flight landed, like she had promised she would. He was headed to a bull riding event in Wyoming and his flight would be in the air by the time hers landed. He said he'd call her as soon as he arrived at the airport.

Somehow she had avoided going to bed with him, but it had not been easy. As badly as she wanted to, she knew she needed to get to know him better.

She'd enjoyed talking with Creed's brothers last night. She

liked all four of his brothers, including Blake, even though he'd been distant. Maybe he had seemed that way because he'd been upset over the woman named Sally.

Creed had wanted to take her to his family's ranch but there hadn't been time for that. She'd had to leave Sunday morning in order to get home and prepare for work on Monday. He'd taken her to the airport and walked with her to the security checkpoint. The kiss he'd given her was beyond amazing and she'd wished she didn't have to leave.

While waiting for her flight, she'd tried to reach Kelsey, but her call went straight to voice mail and she'd had to leave a message.

When she finished showering and had dressed in jean shorts and a T-shirt, she wandered into her living room. It felt lonely not being around Creed, which was crazy since she'd lived alone for some time now. She'd never felt this way while dating anyone. Maybe it was because he was so far away, on the road again.

Her phone rang and she'd picked it up from where she'd left it on the end table by the couch. *Barry* was on the caller ID.

Danica frowned at the phone. When would Barry get the hint? How would she make him get it?

"Barry," she said as she answered the phone, prepared to tell him this had to stop.

"A bull rider?" he said before she had a chance to say anything. "You're seeing some bull rider named Creed McBride?"

"How did you know that?" Danica frowned. Was Barry having her followed?

"Ran into Kelsey this weekend." Barry sounded angry. "She told me you're dating this cowboy."

Kelsey and her big mouth.

But then, Danica thought, this could work in her favor. If Barry knew she wasn't making it up about dating a guy, maybe he would go away.

Not likely.

Danica straightened where she stood. "Yes, I'm seeing Creed."

"I Googled him," Barry said. "He's bad news."

"You did what?" Danica put one hand on her hip. "You have no right butting into my business."

"I do when I care about you," Barry said. "It's all over the place that he goes out on women."

"Don't believe everything you read." Danica's skin flushed hot. "But that's besides the point. I don't want to be around you. I don't even want you calling me." She'd been patient long enough. "Goodbye, Barry. Don't call me again."

"Danica—"

She pressed the *End* button and threw the phone onto the couch. She crossed her arms over her chest and glared at the phone. It rang again with Barry's name coming up, but she ignored it.

Still fuming, she went to the kitchen and cut up an apple and got out some peanut butter and ate them together, one of her favorite comfort snacks. The phone rang two more times and she just stood in the kitchen her hip up against the counter, and ate her apple and peanut butter.

When the phone rang again, she marched into the living room, prepared to turn the damned thing off when she saw the display.

Kelsey.

A measure of relief went through her and she smiled. She picked up the phone. "Hi, Kels."

"Did you have a great trip?" Kelsey said the moment Danica answered. "How were things with Creed? Did you go to bed with him?"

"Whoa." Danica laughed at her friend's rapid-fire questions. "I had a great trip, everything went great, but no, I did not have sex with him."

"Bummer." Kelsey sounded disappointed. "Well, I want to hear all the details that *are* juicy."

Danica sat on the couch and curled her legs beneath her. She told Kelsey about the trip and the time she'd spent with Creed and that they'd almost ended up in bed together.

"I don't get why not," Kelsey said. "You hit it off, you've been talking for a couple of weeks, you're crazy about him, and he's hotter than hell."

"I just don't feel like I know him well enough." Danica paused. "I need more than one weekend with a man before I end up in bed with him. Besides, who says I'm crazy about him?"

"Heh." Kelsey laughed. "The way you talk about him and the fact you flew out to watch him ride in his hometown. Come on, who are you kidding? You're definitely not kidding me."

"Maybe." Danica smiled to herself then laughed. "Okay, I guess you're right." She pushed her hair out of her face. "Why did you tell Barry about Creed?"

"He was at the resort where the wedding was," Kelsey said. "When I bumped into him, he started pelting me with questions about you so I told him that you were seeing someone. I didn't think it would hurt to tell him who you're dating. Was that okay?"

Danica couldn't help but smile at her friend's sincerity. "It was fine, Kels. Better he find out now, I guess. It would be nice if he'd take a hint, though."

"Did you see Darryl?" Kelsey sounded breathy, excited as she changed the subject. "I haven't talked with him since Saturday."

"I need to talk with you about Darryl." Danica paused. "I saw him with another woman."

For a heartbeat Kelsey didn't say anything. "Darryl said his cousin lived there and he'd be seeing her."

"This didn't look like a cousin type of relationship, unless they're kissing cousins," Danica said.

"Darryl wouldn't do that to me." As Kelsey said the words, Danica pictured her friend shaking her head with vehemence. "He cares about me too much. He told me he's in love with me."

Danica bit her lower lip as she gripped the phone.

"You didn't see them kiss, did you," Kelsey stated, her voice rising in pitch.

"Well, no," Danica said. "But the way they looked together—"

"That woman was just his cousin like he told me." Kelsey sounded almost hysterical.

Danica didn't know how to give her friend the rest of the news when she was so adamant about Darryl's fidelity.

"There's something else," Danica said, forcing herself to continue. "I'm going to tell you this because I care too much about you to not tell you." She didn't give Kelsey a chance to respond. "Darryl's been arrested in the past for domestic violence with his ex-wife."

"She lied." Kelsey had an edge to her voice that Danica didn't recognize in her friend. "Darryl told me about it. He said she was angry with him because he wanted a divorce so she made it all up."

Danica felt surprise at the fact that Darryl had brought it up to Kelsey already, but she made herself continue. "Creed said that there are rumors that Darryl is rough with women."

"So now Creed is spreading rumors?" Kelsey was starting to sound angry. "Darryl would never hurt a woman."

Danica clenched the phone. "I'm only telling you these things because I care about you."

"If you cared about me, you'd be happy for me instead of telling me horrible things about Darryl that aren't true." Now Kelsey was practically yelling. "Some friend you are."

A sick feeling settled in Danica's gut. "I'm sorry, Kelsey. I just thought you should know those things."

"I've got to go." Kelsey said. "I'll see you around." Then she hung up.

The sick feeling grew in Danica's belly. Had she been wrong about Darryl? Had Creed? Should she have just shut up and not said anything to Kelsey about it?

Danica lowered the phone to her lap. No, she'd had to tell Kelsey. She might be mad now but it was better that she was at least prepared for the truth.

But Danica didn't think Kelsey was prepared at all. She was in denial, infatuated with a man who could hurt her in so many ways, including physically.

If Kelsey wasn't going to listen to her, Danica wondered if maybe she should have a talk with Darryl Thompson herself.

Danica put her hand to her forehead and closed her eyes. She should probably wait and give Kelsey a chance to cool off and talk with her about it again.

CHAPTER 10

Danica unlocked her front door, relieved to be home after a long day at work. Hell, a long week. It was Friday and she was thrilled it was time for the weekend.

She shut and locked the door behind her, dropped her laptop bag on the couch, hung her purse on the back of a chair, and went into her bedroom where she proceeded to strip out of her work slacks and blouse. She stood in front of the mirror in her hot pink panties and bra and pulled her hair back in a ponytail, then slipped into a pair of jean shorts and a white blouse.

Another week had gone by filled with telephone calls and text messages from Creed. Danica had watched him on TV again just to see him even though she was worried that he'd get hurt. Thankfully he hadn't been. In the last event she watched him in, it was the first time she'd seen him come in with a lower score than Darryl.

And truth was, she missed Creed. She wanted to be with him, spend time with him, and she knew she was crazy for getting involved with a bull rider. It was everything she'd thought it would be—lonely, wanting to be with him while he was on the road, and concerned that he might get seriously injured.

She'd also spent the week avoiding Barry and trying to get in touch with Kelsey who was ignoring her calls. Kelsey had even stopped showing up at the club where they usually met to work out.

The fact that her friend was so hurt made Danica's stomach ache and she'd begun to doubt herself and the choice she'd made to tell Kelsey her suspicions about Darryl. But at the same time, she knew that as Kelsey's friend, she'd had to tell her. Danica hoped she was wrong about Darryl, but her gut told her she wasn't.

There was a knock at the front door just as Danica was heading out of the bedroom and to the kitchen to make dinner. She paused. Was it Barry? He'd stopped by a couple of times and she had peeked out the peephole and hadn't opened the door. If the man couldn't take an outright statement that she didn't want to see him, she wasn't going to mess with it any longer.

The knock sounded again and she went to the door and looked through the peephole. Her eyes widened in surprise when she saw the tall figure in a cowboy hat. Excitement rolled through her as she unlocked the door and opened it.

"Creed." She caught her breath as he stepped in through the door, grasped her around the waist, and pulled her close to him.

He kissed her hard and she gave a sigh of pleasure. When he raised his head he smiled. "Hello, beautiful."

"Hi, cowboy." She wrapped her arms around his neck and he kicked the door shut behind him.

He dropped the duffel he'd been carrying, caught her by the waist, and brought her closer. She pressed her mouth to his and he kissed her again.

His kiss was filled with the same pent-up passion that she felt. She didn't know how much longer she could go without having him…and with him here now that might be impossible to do.

When they drew apart again, she was smiling up at him and looking into his beautiful green eyes. He looked so damned good in a blue western shirt, dark blue Wranglers, and a straw Stetson. He had a day's stubble that looked sexy on him and she breathed in his masculine scent.

"What are you doing here?" She traced her fingers along his stubbled jaw. "Don't you have an event this weekend?"

"Taking this weekend off." He rocked her side to side in his embrace. "I had to see you."

"That's why you drilled me on my plans for the weekend." She laughed. "Pretty sneaky."

"Lucky me that you didn't have any." He smiled. "But now you do."

"Yes, now I do." She slipped her arms from around his neck and placed them on his chest. "I am looking at you but I still can't believe you're here." She smiled at him then gestured toward the kitchen. "Let me get you something to drink. How about a beer or soda? I was just about to fix dinner."

"It was a long flight." He took off his hat and set it on the back of the couch. "A beer sounds great."

Another knock at the door had her tensing. This time she

was certain it was Barry. She drew away from Creed and peeked through the peephole. It was him.

She glanced at Creed and said in a low voice, "It's my ex-boyfriend. He just won't take 'no' for an answer. He won't leave me alone. I am just tired of it."

Creed stepped past her, surprising her as he opened the door. He blocked the doorway and she couldn't see Barry.

"What can I do for you?" Creed asked in a hard voice.

"You're that bull rider," Barry stated, derision in his tone. "Where's Danica?"

"She's busy." Creed had one hand on the doorframe, the other on the doorknob. "Do you have a message for her?"

"I want to see her." Barry sounded angry. "Now."

"I told you, she's busy." Creed's voice had a hard edge to it and his drawl deepened. "If you don't have anything to say then you'd best move on."

"Tell her to call Barry." He spat the words.

"I'll do that." Creed shut the door in Barry's face.

Danica found she was holding her breath and let it out in a slow exhale. She wasn't sure if she should be grateful to Creed or upset with him for taking control like he had. She supposed if it would keep Barry from bothering her, perhaps it had been a good thing.

Maybe she shouldn't like the he-man thing, but for some reason she did. Deep inside she'd liked Creed stepping in and taking control as if she was his woman.

His woman. She nearly groaned at the turn of her thoughts.

He faced her. "If he bothers you again, just let me know."

With a shake of her head, Danica said, "Really, I can take care of him myself." The words were lame because she hadn't been able to get rid of Barry by herself yet. "But thank you."

Creed caught her face in his hands and kissed her. "How about that beer?"

She smiled. "Yes. How about that beer."

CHAPTER 11

Barry glared at the door, his hands fisted at his sides. *That sonofabitch.*

He turned and marched down the front stairs of the townhouse. Fury burned beneath his skin. He'd never been so angry in all his life. All that stood between him and Danica was this bull rider who'd come out of nowhere. Well, he was just going to have to get him out of the way.

He dug his cell phone out of his pocket, pulled up his contacts, and dialed.

"Mac Dawson, private investigator," a woman said when she answered the phone.

"This is Barry Hobbes." He strode to his black Mercedes as he spoke. "Let me speak to Mac."

"Sure, Mr. Hobbes," the woman said. "I'll get him now."

"Barry," the young PI said when he picked up, "what can I do for you?"

Barry unlocked then climbed into his Mercedes. As soon as he started the car, the phone switched over so that the call now came through the car's speakers. "I have a job for you."

"Tell me about it."

"A woman I know is dating a womanizer, a cheat, and a real bastard." Barry scowled as he pulled the car away from the curb and then started down the street. "I want as much dirt dug up on this guy as you can get. Find out who he's seeing, what he's doing."

"What's his name?"

"Creed McBride." Barry clenched the steering wheel. "He's some kind of pro bull rider."

"What else can you tell me about him?" Mac asked.

"That's your job." Barry pulled the car up to a sign at a four-way stop then rolled through when he saw it was clear. "I'll pay whatever it takes. Just get me everything you can."

CHAPTER 12

Danica was thankful Creed didn't seem to want to discuss Barry. Instead she led him to the kitchen where she opened the fridge and brought out two bottles of beer and set them on the counter. She took the magnetic bottle opener off the fridge and popped the cap off of one beer bottle. The cap bounced across the counter and landed on the tile floor with a clatter. He picked it up while she cracked the other bottle open.

"To surprise visits," she said as they bumped their bottles together in a toast. They each took a drink before she lowered her bottle and said, "I'm glad you came."

"Couldn't keep me away from you," he said with sincerity in his voice and in his eyes.

He held her gaze for a long moment and a tingling sensation flowed through her body. She swallowed. "Would you like to go out for dinner or eat in?" She gestured to the fridge. "I have taco makings."

"Tacos sound great." He started rolling up his shirtsleeves. "What can I do to help?"

She loved a man who made himself useful. "You can grate the cheese." She walked to the fridge. "I defrosted some ground beef."

He washed his hands while she got out the cheese, a plate, and the grater for him. She put the ground beef in a frying pan, seasoning it with lots of fresh garlic, salt, ground pepper, and crushed red pepper.

They talked while they made dinner in the same easy way that they always were able to talk to each other. She'd wondered if they'd run out of things to share, but there was always something about their childhoods, their families, their occupations, things they liked to do, places they liked to go.

After dinner they sat on the couch. He was on his third beer and she was drinking her second. She finished it and set the empty on the end table beside her.

He set his own beer bottle aside on the coffee table. "Is this couch where I'm sleeping?" he asked as he put his arm around her shoulders and brought her close. "Or would you prefer I stay in a hotel?"

Flutters erupted in her belly as she met his gaze. His eyes were so intense, so filled with sincerity. Whatever she told him she wanted, she knew he would do it.

She cleared her throat. "You can sleep here."

He reached up and brushed hair from her eyes. "Maybe it's

not a good idea to stay with you after all. I don't know that I can keep my hands off you."

The flutters in her belly increased. Instead of answering she moved her mouth to his, catching him off guard. She kissed him with all the pent up passion inside her and moved in his arms so that she was straddling him on the couch, her knees to either side of his thighs.

She drew back from the kiss, her lips moist and parted, her eyes heavy-lidded as she settled herself more firmly on his lap. With everything she had, she wanted him.

He grasped her waist, his own eyes dark with desire. "Danica, don't start something you aren't going to want to finish."

Danica kissed Creed hard, fierce. He groaned and slid his hands down to her ass and shifted his hips so that his erection was pressed hard against her center. She drew away from his kiss, her breathing deepening.

He slid his hands to her breasts and cupped them as he studied her as if waiting for her to tell him no. Instead, she reached for the top button and started unbuttoning her blouse. He nudged her hands away with his own and took over, slowly undoing each button, his knuckles brushing her soft skin.

She held her breath as her blouse fell open and he palmed her breasts over the satin of her pink bra. A moan escaped her as he fondled her nipples through the soft material. Her throat worked and she had a hard time not closing her eyes and falling into the erotic spell that held them both.

He pushed her blouse over her shoulders and she moved her arms so that the material slid down them and landed on the floor. The air felt cool on her bare skin as he reached behind her and unfastened her bra. With her help he slid it off her arms and tossed it somewhere behind her. He audibly sucked in his breath as he looked at her breasts.

Her nipples tightened beneath his gaze and he teased them with his fingertips as he brought his mouth to hers and kissed her. She sighed as their mouths moved together and he played with her nipples, and she grew even damper between her thighs.

He drew away from her again then lowered his head as he cupped her breasts. He sucked one of her nipples into his warm mouth and she gasped with pleasure, as the tingling between her thighs grew more intense. He moved his mouth to her other nipple and sucked it.

She found herself holding her breath then gasping for air. She slid her fingers into his hair, feeling the soft strands between her fingers as he licked and sucked her nipples. He played with them, teased them, driving her crazy with want and need.

Maybe it was too soon, but inside she felt that this was right. In a matter of weeks, she'd fallen hard for Creed and she wanted everything he could offer her.

He moved his hands to her waist and reached for the button to her shorts. "These have to come off." His voice was husky with desire. He stood, raising her with him. He set her on her bare feet, then unzipped her shorts.

They fell to her ankles. He slipped his fingers into the waist-band of her panties and pushed them over her hips and they landed on her shorts.

He took her by her shoulders as she stepped out of her clothing and his gaze slid over her breasts, down her waist to the trimmed patch of curls between her thighs and on down her long legs. "You are gorgeous, Danica," he murmured. "I want to touch you and taste you everywhere."

When their gazes met again she reached for his shirt and pulled it out of his jeans and started unbuttoning it. Her hands were steady as she focused on her task. She pushed it off his shoulders and he let it slip down to the floor. A light sprinkling of hair covered his powerful chest and every muscle was well defined. Somehow he looked even better than he had the day he'd stepped out of the shower and had come to her with only a towel slung low around his hips, and she never would have thought that possible.

He brought her to him in a rough kiss, like he couldn't wait any longer to touch her. As he continued to kiss her hard, he smoothed his callused palms over her soft skin from her shoulders, down her sides, to her ass and back again. His hands felt warm, the movements slow and erotic.

"Damn but you're beautiful." His jeans were rough against her bare skin as he palmed her ass and jerked her close, his belt buckle digging into her belly. He kissed her again and she rested her hands on his chest, feeling the hard muscles beneath her fingertips.

She slid her fingers down his chest to his tight abs and reached for his belt buckle. She moved back just enough to unfasten his buckle and undo his belt.

"Hold on, honey." He stepped back just enough so that he could remove his boots. The first one hit the floor with a hard *thunk* followed by another when his second boot landed. He unzipped his Wranglers and let them fall to the floor then followed it by removing his boxer briefs and socks.

When he was naked, she grasped his erection in her hand. Long and thick... She loved the feel of the hardness beneath the soft skin. She imagined what he would taste like and what he would feel like inside her.

"Where's your bedroom?" His words came out rough.

She swallowed. "Down the hall, last room on the right."

He scooped her up in his arms and she caught her breath in surprise. She slipped her arms around his neck and held on. His bare skin felt hot next to hers and a thrill went through her belly as he carried her into her room.

He set her on the bed, the comforter soft beneath her back, and then he climbed onto the mattress and straddled her. He kissed her hard then rose up to look into her eyes. "You are an amazing woman, Danica."

"You're not so bad yourself," she said with a smile.

"I want to touch your soft skin forever." He ran a finger between her breasts and down her belly to her bellybutton. "I've wanted to touch you since the moment we met."

She caught her breath as he kissed her again before moving his lips to her chin and trailing them down her neck to the hollow of her throat.

She squirmed beneath him as he eased down her body and licked a path to one of her firm breasts. He teased her nipple with his teeth and tongue then sucked it and lightly dragged at it with his teeth.

With what sounded like a low growl, he kissed a path from her nipple, over the swell of her breast, and down to the valley between her breasts. He eased down her body as he kissed her everywhere she wanted him to.

She slid her fingers into his soft hair as he slid his tongue down the center of her flat belly to the patch of hair between her thighs.

He drew in a deep breath as he nuzzled her curls and pressed her thighs farther apart.

He pressed soft kisses to the insides of her thighs and she sucked in her breath as her legs trembled. But he didn't lick her folds like she'd hoped he would. Instead, he adjusted her so that he could kiss the backs of her knees, causing her to shiver.

Through heavy-lidded eyes, she watched him as he moved in a slow, erotic path all the way down the backs of her calves to her ankles and then her feet.

"Where did you learn how to drive a woman crazy like this?" she said in a soft moan.

He gave a low laugh. "I'm just getting started."

She groaned and her thighs trembled. She was wide open and aching for his mouth on her clit.

Her mind whirled as he drove her crazy with the need to have him. But he kept on teasing her, taunting her while he did the same with her opposite leg, kissing and licking it in the most sensitive places.

Her breathing quickened as he drew out the sensations. And then he was moving up her again. He didn't lick her between her thighs like she wanted. It was as if he was doing it to drive her crazy. If he was trying to do just that, it was working.

He moved up so that he was straddling her shoulders and his cock was in front of her mouth. He grasped his erection in his hand and moved it to her mouth. She parted her lips and he slid his cock into her mouth. He tasted salty and felt warm and big. Slowly moving his hips, he drew his cock in and out. It was an almost helpless feeling with him in control and her obedient to his desires.

His gaze was dark and intense as he watched her. She loved

sucking him as he pushed slowly in to the back of her throat then drew out. He gritted his teeth and she could tell he was close to coming when he pulled out then moved down her body again and adjusted himself so that he could kiss her.

Her lips were wet and he ran his tongue along her upper lip and then her lower. She gave a soft moan, which he took from her when he covered her mouth with his own and kissed her hard.

She wanted him so badly that she couldn't think straight. He pinched her nipples as he kissed her and she writhed with excitement.

"Why are you driving me crazy?" she asked as he drew away from the kiss.

He gave a sexy grin. "Because I can."

She groaned as he moved down her body and eased between her thighs. She was aching and wet and ready.

He slid his palms beneath her ass and raised her up at the same time he moved his mouth to her folds.

With a cry she arched her hips and he pressed his mouth more firmly against her. He licked and sucked her clit and she moaned and moved with every sensation that rocketed through her.

He slid two fingers inside her and pumped them in and out, his knuckles slapping against her flesh. She wondered how much longer she could last with such exquisite pleasure flooding her body.

A climax came rolling toward her, faster and faster. Her skin tingled and her scalp prickled. He increased pressure against her clit and she lost it.

Her body bucked and jerked and she shouted loud and long, unable to think. All she could do was feel as pleasure washed over her in hot waves.

As she came down from the orgasm high she looked up into Creed's eyes. "I left my wallet in your living room and a condom inside it." He kissed her softly, his lips lingering agasint hers before he said, "I'll be right back."

"Wait." Still feeling boneless, she pointed to the nightstand next to her. "Top drawer. A good girl is always prepared."

He gave her a sexy grin then leaned over and pulled the drawer open. A couple of condoms in foil wrappers rested on the side closest to the bed.

The anticipation building inside of her was almost unbelievable in its intensity. She couldn't wait to have him inside her. She watched as he took the condom out of the foil and tossed the wrapper aside. Her heart beat faster as he rolled the condom down the length of his erection.

When he was finished, he grasped her by the waist and surprised her by flipping her over onto her belly. It was nothing like the slow, sensual ride she'd been on so far. Thrills rolled through her as he adjusted her so that she was on her knees, his hand to the back of her neck, her cheek pressed against the comforter.

His cock pushed against the entrance to her core and then he slammed his hips against her, driving his length and thickness inside her.

She cried out at the feel of him stretching her, filling her, and the way he'd driven so deep.

He held himself still for a moment. "Damn, you're tight." He began fucking her hard, his groin slapping against her ass. He adjusted her again and grabbed her hair with one hand and pulled, forcing her to raise her head.

Pain stung at her scalp and tears wet her eyes. Yet at the same time, it felt hot, exciting, wild. He reached around her and started rubbing her clit.

The feel of him taking her while pulling her hair and rubbing her clit was almost sensory overload. Her orgasm came out of nowhere, ripping through her with the power of a freight train.

She screamed. It came out loud and long and it barely registered that the neighbors could probably hear. At that moment she didn't care. All she cared about was the incredible sensations in her body. Her core clenched his cock and her clit throbbed.

If he wasn't holding her head back by her hair, she might have collapsed from exhaustion after having two incredible orgasms.

His hips continued to piston against her backside and then she heard a low growl and then a shout as he came.

She felt his cock pulse inside her as he pulled her hair as if slowing a runaway horse. He pumped his hips a few more times and then let go of her hair and pulled out of her before collapsing onto his side and bringing her with him. He spooned her from behind and she felt his perspiration mingling with hers as they both went limp with exhaustion.

"You are an amazing woman, Danica." He pressed his lips against her cheek and adjusted her so that she was cradled in the crook of his arm.

With a smile she relaxed even more and drifted off as he held her close.

CHAPTER 13

Danica slowed on the elliptical trainer as she began the two-minute cool-down. She'd just completed forty-five minutes on the machine at the health club. Sweat dripped down from her hairline and forehead and she grabbed her hand towel and mopped her face with it. Her T-shirt was damp with perspiration and droplets rolled between her breasts and she dabbed at her chest with the bright yellow towel. She set it aside and continued moving her legs on the machine as she took a long drink out of her water bottle.

She lowered the bottle and smiled to herself as she thought about her incredible weekend with Creed. He'd left last night to head off to his next event and she already missed him. Somehow he'd gotten inside her and she cared for him far more than she wanted to admit.

Not only had they enjoyed each other in bed, but they'd also had fun doing other things. On Saturday they'd spent time at the beach during the day, ate lunch at a crab shack, and that evening had gone out dinner and then to a popular country-western bar. Creed was a great dancer and he enjoyed it, which made it fun for her. On Sunday they'd spend most of the day in her townhouse until he'd had to catch the last flight out to San Antonio.

Her smile faded a bit as she thought about his chosen career and she sighed. A bull rider. What was with some men and the need to put themselves in the midst of danger? It was a question she'd been asking herself over and over. The next question was what was she doing in a relationship with someone like that? Couldn't she have chosen a man with a stable career where his job wasn't out to kill him? Literally.

But she couldn't help how she felt about him. He was easy to talk with and their interests were so similar—with the exception of the bull riding. She liked how genuine he was and how much he seemed to care about her and everything she did from her work to every other aspect of her life. There was little that they hadn't talked about. She felt like nothing was taboo between them and she wondered if he felt the same way.

The machine she was on beeped, telling her that she'd completed her workout. The numbers of minutes and miles flashed across the screen. She stepped off the elliptical trainer, grabbed her towel and water bottle, and headed across the gym toward the women's locker room. She'd done weights and core before the elliptical and felt pumped from her workout.

She came to a stop when she saw a familiar figure walking through the front door.

"Kelsey." Danica jogged up to her friend. Usually they worked out together, but since Kelsey had been avoiding her that hadn't been the case. Today Danica had come in later than usual and she was glad to see her friend.

Kelsey came up short, a hesitant expression on her face. She hadn't taken off her big sunglasses even though she was now inside the gym. She was carrying her gym bag and was still in street clothes.

Danica went up to Kelsey, wishing she could see her eyes so that perhaps she could tell what her friend was thinking. "Can we talk?" Danica asked.

Kelsey bit her lower lip then shrugged. "All right."

"Let's go in the locker room." Danica gave a nod in that direction.

They walked toward the women's side of the locker rooms and Danica dabbed her damp forehead with the workout towel. The clanging of weights, the whir of exercise machines and pulsing music surrounded them. It was a small, older health club with more male members than female, and it smelled of sweat and testosterone.

When they reached the women's locker room, Danica sat on one of the benches near the lockers and looked up at Kelsey who was still standing. She hesitated then sat at the opposite side of the bench and set her gym bag by her feet.

"We need to talk about last week," Danica said. "I felt I needed to tell you those things because you're my closest friend. I don't want to see you hurt."

Kelsey said nothing and looked at a wall. She wore light pink lipstick and her long blonde hair hung in soft curls around her face, but the sunglasses she still wore hid her pretty gray eyes. For some reason she looked petite and vulnerable.

"Can you take those off?" Danica tilted her head slightly. "It's hard to talk to you when I can't see your eyes."

Again Kelsey hesitated but then she reached up and slowly took off the sunglasses.

Danica sucked in her breath. One side of Kelsey's face was bruised and swollen, and she had a black eye. She'd tried to cover it up with makeup but there was no disguising the fact that she'd been hit.

"Did Darryl do that to you?" Danica could barely get the words out as fury began to make her hands shake.

Kelsey shook her head. "I ran into a door." The response sounded planned, not natural, not to mention unbelievable.

"Some door," Danica said and she could hear the disbelief in her own tone. "If Darryl touched you, I'm going to rip him apart."

"Darryl is a good man. He wouldn't do anything to hurt me." Kelsey's lower lip trembled but she sat up straighter. "I love him."

Trying to control herself, Danica looked down at the hand towel she was gripping in her fist then met Kelsey's gaze again.

"I don't want anything to happen to you." Danica reached out and put her hand on Kelsey's. "You are my closest friend and you're like a sister to me. Please understand that and know that you can talk to me about anything."

Kelsey pulled her hand away and her expression hardened. "There's nothing wrong between Darryl and me." Kelsey got to her feet and picked up her sunglasses. "I need to work out now."

Danica straightened, her heart aching at the same time her blood boiled. She stood. "Will you be here at our usual time on

Wednesday?"

With a shrug, Kelsey said, "I'm not sure. Work has been rough lately."

"Okay." Anger at Darryl still burned inside Danica but she forced a smile. "I've missed you, Kels."

The hard look that had been on Kelsey's face melted a little. "I've missed you, too."

Danica reached for Kelsey, hugged her, then drew away. "Why don't we go out for lunch on Friday?"

"All right." Kelsey smiled but it looked like it hurt a bit because she winced.

Inwardly, Danica winced, too. "I'll call you Thursday."

Kelsey nodded. "Okay." She picked up her gym bag and went to one of the lockers. Without looking back at Danica, she started changing out of her street clothes and into her workout shorts and T-shirt.

Danica went to her own locker and unlocked the combination lock, her hands shaking from the strength of her anger. She grabbed her bag with everything in it, threw the lock inside, and shut the empty locker. She paused a moment as she looked at Kelsey's rigid backside.

"See you Thursday for workout," Danica said. "Or Friday for lunch, whichever comes first."

Kelsey looked over her shoulder. "See you," she said before turning away again.

Danica started to leave the locker room. She looked back once at Kelsey's bent head then turned and walked out.

As she headed out of the club, Danica's mind turned over and over the fact that Kelsey had been hit and she was certain that

Darryl had been the one to do it.

If she confronted Darryl about it, he could go back to Kelsey and become more violent with her.

Frustrated, angry, and concerned for her friend, Danica pushed her hand through her hair. She couldn't just stand by and watch her friend be abused.

But what should she do?

She narrowed her eyes. When she went to the Sonoita event in two weeks Darryl was sure to be there... And she was going to have a talk with him.

CHAPTER 14

Just as Barry walked into his home, his cell phone rang. He drew it out of his pocket and checked the caller ID screen.

Mac Dawson.

Barry shut the door behind him and answered, "What do you have for me, Mac?"

"Plenty." The PI sounded satisfied. "Creed McBride is having an affair with some blonde. When I called you last, you did say the woman you're protecting from him is a brunette."

"Yes." Barry's mood elevated as he set his car keys on the small table in the foyer. "Tell me what you have."

"They had dinner together and ended up in her hotel room," Mac said. "He was there a couple of hours but didn't spend the night. Next morning he returned to the hotel, was there about an hour, and then they went to breakfast. They returned to the hotel room after breakfast. I've got pictures of him coming and going and the date and time is on every picture."

"Excellent." A sense of elation went through Barry. He had the sonofabitch and he had him good. "Who's the woman?"

"I haven't found out who she is yet," Mac said, "but when they're alone they are an intimate little couple. The photos prove it."

Barry walked through his spacious and elegant home to his office and sat behind his desk where his laptop was set up. "E-mail the pictures to me."

"You should already have them," Mac said. "I'm sending over hard copies by courier now."

Barry pulled up his email program and found the message from Mac. He clicked on the zip folder attachment, opened it, and started clicking on each photo.

McBride was with a woman in each of the photos. Definitely not Danica. He was talking with the blonde, holding her, and the last photograph was of him with his forehead against hers in what looked like a tender moment.

A smile crept across Barry's face as he looked at the photos with satisfaction. "What else can you tell me?"

Mac proceeded to tell him what he saw, where the couple met, and that he knew the woman would be at the next event, too. He had dug up info about McBride's past conquests, as well.

"I'm not finished with the investigation and I'm still on McBride's trail," Mac said. "He's on the move traveling the bull riding circuit, so it's not as easy as it would be if I could catch him in one place, like his hometown."

Barry frowned. "How did you get all of the information that you do have?"

"You pay me good money to get the info," Mac said. "Don't ask me how."

"Yes, I'm paying you good money." Irritation prickled Barry's skin. "So I'd like an answer to my question."

"Some old-fashioned investigative work," Mac said smoothly, still evading a direct answer. "I'll get those photographs to you ASAP, and when the job is completed I'll provide you with a written report."

Barry disconnected the call and clicked through the photographs on his computer again. These would show Danica that McBride was nothing but a cheating bastard.

With smug satisfaction, Barry leaned back in his chair and looked at the photographs of McBride with the woman. Danica would see that Barry cared enough about her to investigate the cowboy and realize that the bull rider wasn't the one for her.

She'd know the truth of it, that Barry loved her and wanted the best for her. She deserved much better than McBride, and she would see that Barry was that man.

CHAPTER 15

A fluttering sensation teased Danica's belly as she drove the white Mustang she'd rented from an agency at the airport in Tucson. Moments later, she entered Sonoita where Creed had already arrived.

Her thoughts turned to Barry for a moment. He'd left her a voice mail yesterday, saying he had something important to tell her about her "bull rider boyfriend." She'd deleted the message. Whatever Barry had to say, she really didn't care. She shoved thoughts of him out of her mind. She intended to have a great time with Creed and not think about Barry at all.

Red, white, and blue banners fluttered around the area with signs announcing the annual rodeo and new bull riding event that would take place over the weekend. How things had changed over the last couple of years. Then she would never have thought that Sonoita would have the capacity to draw in enough people for the professional bull riding organization's championship circuit.

Up ahead was the small inn where Creed had stayed last night. After meeting up with him, they would go to her brother's ranch in the San Rafael Valley, about twenty-five minutes from Sonoita.

After she pulled the car up to the inn, she turned off the engine, climbed out, and stretched her legs. It was good to be out of the car and drinking in the fresh air in the small town that was no bigger than a village.

The inn looked like it could've been from the Old West, and the wooden steps and porch creaked beneath her boots. She wore jeans, a button-up red blouse, and her long dark hair fell loose around her shoulders.

A warm summer breeze stirred her hair and cooled her skin at the same time. Anticipation at seeing Creed again lightened her steps.

Just as she was about to walk into the inn, Darryl stepped out of the doorway.

Danica came to an abrupt stop. She hadn't expected to come face to face with him so soon. Now was as good a time as any to have a talk with him.

"Danica, right?" Darryl said in a Texas drawl and he gave her a grin. "I'd remember a cute little thing like you, anywhere."

"Kelsey is my closest friend." Danica tilted her chin. "I want to talk to you about her."

He raised an eyebrow. "What about?"

Danica clenched her fists at her sides. "I know you hit her."

"Did she tell you that?" He gave her a long, dark look. "I

would never touch her in that way."

"No, she didn't tell me. She said she ran into a door." Danica clenched her hands into fists. "But I know it was you."

Darryl's expression darkened. "That's a mighty strong accusation. And one that isn't a damned bit true."

"You'd just better keep your hands off Kelsey." Danica narrowed her gaze as anger rolled through her, hot and thick.

His scowl almost had her stepping back but she stood her ground. He looked as if he wanted to hit her and could barely restrain himself. He gave her one last glare then turned and walked away, down the street.

Danica took a deep breath and pushed hair off her forehead. She watched him stride away and head to a parked truck. He climbed into the truck, started the engine and headed out toward the arena.

She leaned back against the wall behind her and looked up at the aged wood covering the porch that ran the length of the building. She needed to calm down before she saw Creed. She didn't want him seeing her upset.

When she had cooled off as much as she could, she called Creed on her cell phone. "I'm here." She turned her thoughts from Darryl and put a smile in her voice.

"Be right there."

Her heart pounded a little faster as she waited for him. A few moments later he walked through the inn's doorway.

He wore a sexy smile that made her belly do flips and his straw Stetson was low over his forehead, shadowing his green eyes. His broad shoulders and muscular arms filled out the blue shirt he was wearing and his Wrangler jeans molded his hips and thighs. He was carrying a black duffel bag with sponsor insignia patches on it.

She smiled at him as he brought her into his arms and kissed her. It had been two weeks since she'd seen him, but it seemed even longer. His kiss was deep and powerful and when he drew away, the sensation of his mouth against hers lingered on her lips.

"I missed you." He touched her cheek. "I don't like being separated from you like this."

"Well, unless you settle down, I guess this is how it's going to be," she said, then realized how that might sound. As if she wanted him to settle down with her, which wasn't what she'd meant at all. Was it?

He smiled, like he was certain that she cared for him enough to think about what it might be like to always be with him. Truth was she had been thinking about that, but with him traveling like he did, and being in the sport he was in, she didn't know how it would ever work.

Setting those thoughts aside, she reached out and hooked her finger in one of his. "Are you ready?"

"Yep." He indicated the bag over his shoulder. "My riding gear is stored, so I've got everything I need here."

"Good." She released his finger and turned to head back to the Mustang. She popped open the trunk and he tossed his bag in beside hers.

He plucked the car keys from her fingers and gave her a little grin. "I like to be in control."

"I've noticed." She shook her head but she really didn't mind. He opened the passenger side door for her and she slid into her seat. He shut the door behind her then strode to the driver's side and climbed in.

As he backed the car away from the inn, she gave him directions to her brother's house.

"So they're not going to mind a little extra company?" Creed asked.

"Not at all." She shook her head. "It's a big house and Jessie and Zane like company."

While they drove, she thought about Kelsey. Her friend hadn't shown up to work out on Thursday and had canceled lunch on Friday. The only thing she'd said was that she wasn't feeling well and she'd cut the conversation short. Danica hadn't talked about it with Creed yet because she knew he'd confront Darryl and she'd wanted to be the one to do that.

Now that she had told him to leave Kelsey alone, she wondered if she should tell Creed. She had a feeling he'd go after Darryl and he'd end up getting into a fistfight and maybe even charged with assault. She needed to think it over a little more before she said anything.

"What's going on in that pretty head of yours?" Creed asked as she looked out the window. "You're not usually so quiet."

"Work." She offered him a smile. "There's a lot going on." At least that was the truth, there was a lot going on.

He gave a nod. "What are you working on now?"

She told him about the new project she'd just started and he asked questions, showing his interest and his understanding of what it was that she did.

It seemed like no time and they were pulling up to the Bar C ranch. Danica and her four brothers had grown up in the huge ranch house that Zane had inherited. Danica, Wayne, Wyatt, and Dillon had each inherited a portion of Cameron lands as well as large sums. Danica had leased her property to Zane as rangelands for his cattle and she had banked her cash. She'd always planned on returning one day and building a house on her property. She just wasn't ready for that yet.

"So this is where you grew up." Creed studied the sprawling home as they passed under the sign with the Bar C's name and brand. The Mustang's wheels rattled over the cattle guard. "Nice."

"It was great growing up here." She smiled as she looked at the native oaks and the stately sycamore trees shading the house. Flowerbeds had been planted in front of the long enclosed porch that ran the length of the house and the colorful flowers danced in the summer breeze. Inside the screened porch was a white loveseat porch swing along with other furniture, and potted plants that Jessie had kept up since she had married Zane.

To the right, an old wooden wagon wheel was propped up against an oak with flowers sprouting around the wheel. A triangular dinner bell hung from one of the lower branches of the oak. On the other side of the house was a covered swing beneath the shade of several old sycamores. The swing was next to a pond with a small waterfall.

On top of the right side of the roof was an old rooster weather vane and behind the house rose a weathered windmill. She imagined the squeaks and scraping sounds the windmill made as the blades turned with the wind.

They pulled up to the house and Creed killed the engine. The front door opened and a pretty red-haired woman carrying a little girl on her hip stepped out through the screen door and headed toward the Mustang. Behind her was a tall dark cowboy.

Danica was out of the car and hurrying toward Jessie and

Zane before Creed had a chance to come around to her side and help her out. The pretty redhead had a cute grin and her body was even more curvaceous after having had a child.

"Jessie." Danica hugged her sister-in-law. "So good to see you." Then Zane embraced her in a tight squeeze.

"Good to have you home," Jessie said.

Zane gave a nod. "About damned time," he said and Danica laughed.

"Let me see Chelsea." Danica held out her arms and took the redheaded two-year-old from Jessie.

Chelsea gave a broad smile. "Aunt Dani!"

Danica kissed the girl's cheek then turned to Creed who had come up behind her. "Creed, this is my sis-in-law, Jessie, my brother, Zane, and my niece, Chelsea." She looked from Jessie to Zane and gestured to Creed. "This is Creed McBride."

Creed took Jessie's hand and gave her a smile then shook hands with Zane who was giving him an appraising look. Danica wanted to punch her brother in the shoulder. She was a grown woman and her brothers were still on the watch for her when it came to men.

"Come on in." Jessie made a gesture toward the house.

Danica carried Chelsea on her hip as they walked. Their boots thumped on the hardwood floor as they entered the home that was spacious and open with high-vaulted ceilings. The western artwork and décor had been their mother's doing before she passed away, but Jessie had added her touches, too, which made the house even homier. Jessie was a photographer and everywhere there were pictures of family, especially Chelsea.

In front of a huge entertainment center and a big screen TV

was a long leather L-shaped couch and another fabric couch with a western design. The views were incredible from the front and back through the big picture windows. She'd loved growing up here and missed it.

"We've got iced tea, lemonade, and munchies to eat for now. Zane is going to fire up the grill," Jessie said and they followed her. "Everyone else will be here soon."

"By everyone else I'm assuming you mean all our brothers and sisters-in-law?" Danica asked with a smile as she held Chelsea.

"Every last one of them." Jessie went to the counter and picked up a couple of bowls of dip. "Can you grab the chips and pretzels?" she asked.

Chelsea squirmed. "I want down."

"Say please," Jessie said as she held the bowls.

"Please," the two-year-old said clearly.

"There you go." Danica set Chelsea on her feet.

Chelsea smiled as she looked up at Danica. "Thank you," she said before running to her father and shouting, "Daddy!" Zane opened his arms and scooped his daughter then tossed her up about a foot. The little girl squealed with laughter and said, "Again, Daddy! Again!"

Creed picked up bowls of potato and corn chips and Danica grabbed the pretzels. They followed Jessie out to the back porch where two long picnic tables were already set up.

The doorbell rang and Jessie hurried to answer it. Zane set Chelsea down and she started chasing a butterfly around the spacious backyard on the lush grass.

One after another everyone arrived and Danica introduced Creed to each of them. Her twin brothers Wayne and Wyatt and their wives, Kaitlyn and Sabrina, were first. Kaitlyn was very pregnant, her and Wayne's baby due any time.

Next came Dillon and his wife, Carly.

To a one her brothers looked Creed over. Dillon recognized him.

"It is sure nice to meet you, Creed," Dillon said. "I've seen you ride a lot over the years. Winning a world championship a couple of times is an amazing feat."

Creed nodded. "Well, thank you."

Danica didn't know if that would win points for him or lose them. Who knew what men had going on in their heads sometimes?

The five men all stood near the grill with her brothers asking Creed questions about bull riding, where he was from, and what else he did besides bull riding.

Danica watched Creed. He looked comfortable and at ease with being around her family. Her brothers' scrutiny and protectiveness didn't seem to faze him at all.

After dinner, Chelsea brought Creed a flower she'd picked. "For you," she said.

He grinned and crouched down so that he was eyelevel with Chelsea. "Thank you." He took the bright yellow flower that she offered him.

Danica watched as he spent time with Chelsea, listening to her chatter and talking to her. She smiled. He would make a good father some day. The thought sent queer feelings through her belly. Creed as the father to her child... She could picture him with a dark-haired little girl or a boy. Could see him teaching them to ride their bikes, play baseball, and ride a horse.

No bull, though. She couldn't handle a bull rider son.

Her insides stirred at the thought of really having a family with Creed.

It was almost as if Creed had heard her thoughts. He raised his head and looked at her and then she couldn't read his expression. It took her aback for a moment. He held her gaze then turned back to Chelsea and smiled at her.

What had that been all about? Had he guessed at the feelings and thoughts running through her?

Where had those thoughts come from, anyway? A father who toured the circuit wouldn't be home long enough to be the kind of husband and father that she was looking for.

She groaned inwardly. This was all just crazy.

The afternoon went well and by that evening, it looked as though her brothers liked Creed, which was a relief to Danica. Her brothers' approval mattered to her more than she liked to admit.

They played horseshoes in the backyard while it was still light, then went in the house and played poker well into the night after Chelsea had been put to bed. The huge dining room table fit ten, which worked out perfectly for the four Cameron brothers and their wives, along with Danica and Creed.

The exciting news of the night was that both Sabrina and Carly were pregnant and due within weeks of each other. They'd both held off waiting to announce it until the whole family was together. Carly and Sabrina had been close friends long before they met two of the Cameron brothers.

While she sat next to Creed, Danica wondered what it would be like to be pregnant with his child. The thought came out of nowhere and her cheeks warmed when Creed asked her what she was thinking about because she'd gone quiet.

"Thinking about how I'm going to kick butt at this game tonight," she said.

Her brothers laughed. "Danica is a force to be reckoned with in just about everything, including poker," Wyatt said. "You've got to watch out for her."

Creed smiled at Danica. "Oh, believe me, I am."

CHAPTER 16

Danica cringed as a raging bull trampled on the last bull rider of the day. A "wreck" the announcers called them each time something happened like this. She wanted to cover her eyes but she made herself watch. If she was going to be with Creed, she had to come to terms with the fact that he could be the next one beneath the bull's hooves.

She shifted on the wooden seat where she sat between a man whose belly was spilling over the top of his big gold and silver belt buckle, and a pair of giddy teenagers who looked like they were buckle bunnies in the making.

As the bullfighters managed to get the bull out of the ring, the cowboy was helped to his feet. He let the men assisting him know that he was all right and then got out of the ring on his own power.

The crowd cheered and the bull rider waved his hat at everyone.

Her phone rang and she dug it out of her jeans pocket and answered it almost absently.

"Danica," Barry said the moment she answered. "I need to talk with you."

Damn it. Why didn't she look at the caller ID?

She blew out a breath. "Barry, I really don't have time—"

"Your cowboy is cheating on you," Barry said. "I have proof."

Heat flooded Danica. A combination of shock at what Barry had said, and anger that he was somehow spying on Creed.

Creed wouldn't cheat on her. There had to be a simple explanation.

"I don't believe you, Barry." Danica shook her head. "As a matter of fact, I want you to stay out of my life. Don't call me, don't stop by, don't contact me in any way."

"Dani—" he started but she pressed the *off* button and severed the connection.

"Bastard," she mumbled under her breath. She was sick and tired of him. She'd tried to break it off gently, then had been direct but still friendly on more than one occasion. Then she'd started ignoring his calls and wouldn't answer the door when he stopped by.

Obviously he didn't get it and likely never would.

The wrap up of the event seemed to take a while, but maybe that was because her mind kept turning over what Barry had said. And she continued to tell herself that Barry was wrong. She knew in her heart that Creed would never do that to her.

When it was over, she got up from the wooden bench seat, brushed off her bottom with her palms, then headed down the steps and out of the stands.

After moving with the crowd leaving the arena, she paused mid-step, trying to remember where she was supposed to meet Creed. She continued on and walked toward the bullpens.

She came to a full stop when she caught sight of Creed. He was with the same blonde woman who'd been in the bar in Las Vegas, the same one he'd talked to in Prescott.

The heat that had flooded her earlier returned. Was Barry right? Could Creed be having an affair?

No. Creed wouldn't do that to her.

Would he?

She hated the doubt now in her mind, but she couldn't shake it as she watched Creed with the blonde. They were walking together and talking and then they disappeared around the side of a building.

A light breeze stirred Danica's hair and she pushed wisps of it out of her face. She had never been an insecure woman who jumped to conclusions. There had to be a reason why he was talking with the blonde.

She waited for Creed to come back outside. A few people she knew came by and she gave each one a wave and one stopped to chat with her for a moment.

When Creed finally came out, carrying his gear, she went up to him. He kissed her hard then drew back and grinned. His grin lessened a bit as he asked, "Is something wrong?"

She shook her head and smiled. "Not at all."

With a nod he indicated the direction where the Mustang was parked. "Ready to go?"

"Ready when you are."

As they walked, a part of her wanted to ask him about the woman, but she didn't want to come off as jealous or demanding. She needed to continue trusting him.

He put his arm around her shoulders as they walked and she leaned into him. "Nice ride today," she said.

"Wasn't enough to take first," he said, "but the points were still a boost to my overall total." He took her hand with his free one and squeezed it. "Ready to head on home?"

She shrugged as she realized she wasn't ready. She wanted to spend time with Creed. A weekend here and there just wasn't enough.

"Hey." He released her hand and put an arm around her shoulders. "I can head to San Diego after this weekend in New Mexico. Do you have time in the middle of the week? That way I can come out between events."

She met his gaze. "Evenings are free but days I have to work. I've already taken off time and don't have much left." She couldn't find it in herself to smile. "This is hard, Creed. Never knowing when I'll see you again and always worrying about you."

He looked thoughtful. "We'll figure out something."

She rested her head against his shoulder as they walked. "I hope so."

* * * * *

Danica sat at a small table in Starbucks as she reviewed a project for work on her iPad. She stopped at the coffee shop most mornings before she went to work and had a caramel macchiato, her favorite.

It was the Thursday following her weekend in Sonoita with her family and Creed. She missed him more than she wanted to admit. A lot more.

She was lost in thought when someone sat across from her. She looked up and saw that it was Barry.

"We need to talk," he said as he set a manila envelope on the table between them.

She let out a sigh of frustration. "The only thing I'm interested in is you agreeing that we're just friends. If not, then we have nothing to talk about."

"I know you are angry with me," Barry said with a sincere expression. "But I care about you and I don't want you with the wrong man."

"I've heard enough." She got to her feet as he pulled an eight by ten black and white photo out of the envelope. She went still.

It was a photograph of Creed with the blonde woman that she'd been seeing him with. He had his forehead to hers and it looked like an intimate moment.

Her face started to burn and her skin prickled as Barry laid one photograph down after another of Creed and the woman.

As Barry laid them down, he pointed to dates and times on each photo of Creed and the blonde. Her knees nearly gave out and she sat in her seat again. She wanted to deny what she was seeing, what she was hearing, but nothing made sense anymore.

"How did you get these?" Her words came out in a near whisper.

"Something about the guy made me worry about you." Barry sounded sincere. "I hired a PI to follow him and this is what he saw." He pointed to each photograph. "This one shows them at dinner, and this one shows them going into her hotel." He gestured to the next one. "If you look at the timestamps, you'll see that he leaves about two hours after he goes in with her."

Danica's mind spun. This couldn't be right, Creed wouldn't do that to her.

But there it was in black and white. He was with another woman on dates that were the same as his last event.

She sat back in her chair, her chest aching, a lump in her throat. Pain like she'd never before experienced tore at her.

Then anger began to rise, anger so great that she shook with it. "I want the photos," she said as she looked at one of the pictures. Her stomach churned as she reached for them.

Barry didn't stop her. "I'm sorry," he said. When she met his gaze, he did look apologetic and she wondered if that was real emotion, or just for her benefit.

"I need to go." She grabbed her iPad along with the pictures, and shoved them all into her purse. She didn't know if she should thank him or yell at him, so she said nothing. She picked up her mostly full cup of macchiato then strode from the table and threw it in the garbage.

Tears bit at the backs of her eyes as she shoved open the door to the coffee shop and a single tear escaped and rolled down her cheek. She brushed it away with a rough, jerky motion as she walked to her car.

Damn him. *Damn him.*

He'd taken her heart and all along he'd been playing her.

She unlocked her car door and jerked it open before climbing behind the wheel and starting the car. She wondered if she should even be driving as angry as she was.

The tires squealed as she spun the car into traffic and headed to work when she'd rather hunt down Creed and let him have it.

CHAPTER 17

Danica had always been a strong woman, but it felt like her world was falling apart. She tried to focus on her anger but she couldn't help the overwhelming thoughts of sadness. It was like someone had died. She'd thought she knew Creed but he wasn't the person she'd thought he was. That person was gone.

Almost as soon as she walked through the door after work, Creed called. She bit the inside of her lip and tried to hold back tears. She knew she had to talk to him sooner or later, but it would have to be later. She wasn't ready to have a conversation with him so she sent his call to voice mail.

Her heart squeezed and teardrops rolled down her cheeks. She had managed to hold back the tears while at work but now they wouldn't stop. She was furious while at the same time she felt totally crushed. Her body felt heavy and she collapsed onto the couch and didn't want to get up.

Teardrops continued to roll down her cheeks. She needed to talk with someone, to get it all out. But Kelsey wasn't talking to her and if she discussed it with any of her brothers they would likely go after Creed and end up in jail.

Danica's phone rang again and she glanced at the caller ID, ready to send Creed or Barry to voice mail if either one of them was calling. It was a San Diego number she didn't recognize.

When she answered the call, a woman on the other end said, "Is this Danica Cameron?"

"Yes." Danica wiped tears from her eyes with the back of her hand, suddenly feeling like something was very wrong. "Who is this?"

"I'm Sarah, a nurse at San Diego General," the woman said. Danica's gut twisted as the woman continued. "Kelsey Richards was admitted an hour ago and she listed you as next of kin."

Shock went through Danica. "What happened? Is she all right?"

"She was physically abused by her boyfriend," the nurse said. "She needs someone to pick her up when we're finished treating her."

"I'll be right there." Danica got instructions on where to go as she grabbed her purse and headed back out the front door, locking it behind her. Her tears dried, her focus solely on Kelsey.

She'd kill Darryl. First chance she got she was going to hurt the bastard right where it counted.

When she finally got to the room at the hospital where Kelsey was being treated, her heart squeezed at the sight of her friend and she almost started crying again. Kelsey's pale face was bruised even more than it had been, her eye was swollen shut, a bandage was on her forehead, and her arm was in a sling.

"Oh, my God." Danica rushed to Kelsey who was in a hospital gown and sitting on the edge of the hospital bed. "Where is Darryl? When I get a hold of him—"

"He's in jail." Kelsey's voice sounded a little scratchy. "I picked him up from the airport and we went to my apartment. Before we were even inside, he slammed me up against the wall beside my front door in the stairwell, yelling at me for telling you about the last time he'd attacked me. When he started hitting me, the neighbor looked out her window and saw it. She dialed 9-1-1 and the cops came and arrested him."

"He's so lucky he's in jail." Danica stroked the side of Kelsey's face that wasn't bruised. "I swear I'd hurt him."

"I'm lucky the neighbor saw it." Kelsey sighed. "You were right all along. I just cared about him so much that the first time he hit me I convinced myself it was an accident. I couldn't come to terms with the fact that he'd abused me. I almost felt like I'd deserved it."

Danica frowned. "You'd better get that thought right out of your head."

"Believe me, it's gone." Kelsey adjusted herself on the edge of the bed and winced when she moved her arm. "I'm pressing charges."

"It's a good thing you are." Danica squeezed Kelsey's good shoulder. "You and I would be having a serious talk if you didn't."

"I'm not going to be a doormat for anyone, anymore." Kelsey set her mouth in a firm line as Danica sat beside her on the edge of the bed. "It finally hit me that I don't deserve this. I don't know why it took me so long."

"Sometimes it's hard to see things about ourselves and about the people we care about." Danica's stomach churned as she thought about Creed. "Sometimes those people aren't who we thought they were after all."

"You've got that right." Kelsey gave a rueful smile. "I think I've finally learned my lesson."

You and me both, Danica thought. *You and me both.*

* * * * *

After she got Kelsey safely home, Danica went home to her townhouse. She got ready for bed, her heart heavy after all that had happened.

When she sat on her bed in her long nightshirt, she made herself look at the photos of Creed and the woman again. There was no brushing this off as nothing. It was clear by the dates and timestamps that he'd spent time with her in her hotel room as well as going out with her to various places.

Fresh anger rushed through her body. How could he do this to her?

When it came down to it, it was her fault for trusting him. She'd seen the evidence on the Internet and in the magazine. She'd just wanted to believe in him so badly.

Her phone rang and she picked it up off the nightstand. It was Creed, his third call since she'd first walked into her home earlier in the afternoon.

She took all the anger, hurt, and sadness inside her and held onto it as she answered the call.

"What's wrong, Danica?" he said when he obviously heard the edge in her tone.

"I know you're having an affair." Her voice was hard as she spoke. "You and I are through."

"What are you talking about?" He sounded genuinely puzzled. "I'm not having any kind of affair."

Great actor, she thought.

"I've been given proof." She picked up one of the pictures and almost crumpled it in her hand. "You and the blonde I've been seeing you with. It's here in black and white."

"Are you talking about Teri?" he said. "I can explain—"

"No, you can't." Danica clenched her cell phone tighter as she cut through his words. "Don't ever call me again. Don't email me. Don't come to my house. Stay. Away. From. Me."

"Danica, wait—"

She disconnected the call then turned her phone off.

The moment her phone was off, tears began rolling down her cheeks and she sobbed so hard that she hiccupped. She held the back of her hand to her mouth to hold back more. An ache so great, like she'd never felt before, sat hard in her chest.

Tears wouldn't stop rolling down her cheeks and she couldn't stop sobbing. Teardrops landed on the photographs of Creed with the blonde. She almost shredded the pictures but she would need them to remind herself of what a bastard he was.

And then, once the tears stopped for good, it would be time to burn them.

CHAPTER 18

On the following day, Friday, Danica stood in her living room, in front of her TV. Creed was in New Mexico for his next event and competing sometime during the next hour or so.

She picked up her remote control as she stared at the TV.

He had called no less than six times. She kept her phone on vibrate while she was at work and it kept going off in her pocket. It had stopped about an hour ago, probably because he was getting ready for his ride tonight.

The only call she's answered that day had been Kelsey's, who was feeling better but still shaken. Danica had wanted to tell her friend about Creed's betrayal, but Kelsey didn't need to have to face anymore negativity than she was already experiencing after yesterday's assault. The discussion about Creed could wait.

She looked at the remote in her hand. What was she doing? Was she seriously considering watching him ride?

It was like she couldn't stop herself. She clicked the TV on then went to the channel the event would be shown on. Two announcers were giving a sort of "pre-game" talk while at the same time cameras went to a bull rider preparing to ride.

She took a deep breath. She needed to do this. Needed to remind herself of every single reason why it was good that she was no longer seeing Creed. At least that was what she told herself.

Still holding the remote, she sank onto the couch as the first bull of the night shot out of the chute, the rider on its back.

She caught her breath as the rider was bucked off of the bull. It never ceased to affect her when the riders were tossed or ended up near the bull's hooves. The bull rider jogged safely out of the arena as the bull headed down a chute.

One after another she watched the riders battle with their bulls until it was Creed's turn. The announcers said that he was to ride a bull by the name of The Machine.

Her belly clenched as her gaze was glued to Creed. She couldn't have taken her eyes off of him if she tried.

Everything about him had been dear from his very presence to the way he seated himself on the bull and prepared himself. She had to get past thinking that way about him, but it was harder than she could ever have imagined it would be.

She held her thumb over the *off* button on the remote. She shouldn't watch, she shouldn't watch, she shouldn't—

The bull exploded out of the chute like nothing she'd ever seen before

It seemed to be in a frenzy as it bucked and twisted round and round. She held her breath as Creed hung on. His ride wasn't as smooth as normal, like he was having a much harder time hanging on.

Just as the eight-second horn sounded, the bull flung Creed off. He hit the ground hard on his back and the bull charged him.

Before he could get out of the way, the bull rammed its head against Creed, hitting him square in the chest and knocking him back.

Danica put her hand over her mouth, covering a scream as she watched in horror.

The bull trampled Creed. It's rear hooves came up high and it slammed them down on Creed's chest.

He was completely still.

"No." Danica shook her head as tears flowed down her cheeks. "Get up, Creed. *Get up!*"

The bull trampled Creed again before the bullfighters finally got its attention, putting themselves in danger while getting the bull away from Creed.

The moment the bull was safely out of the arena, a group of men surrounded Creed who lay unmoving on the ground. The crowd was silent.

Danica felt as if her world was tilting upside down. Was he going to die?

Thoughts whirled through her mind. Even though he had cheated on her, she was in love with him. Being with him when he needed her was more paramount than anything at this moment.

The announcers talked rapid-fire about what everyone had just witnessed and what they were seeing now.

A stretcher was rushed to Creed's side and he was carefully

lifted onto it. He still didn't move.

Danica's hands shook as she ran to her laptop that was sitting out on the coffee table. She had to go to him. She pulled up the site for the airline she normally used, and booked a flight for Albuquerque. She printed out the ticket and went to throw a few things in her backpack.

The announcers were still going on in the background about the seriousness of Creed's injuries as she hurried to grab everything she would need for a quick trip, then rushed out the door, locking it behind her.

Her mind spun with images of what she'd seen, words that the announcers had been saying, and the terror and helplessness of what she was experiencing now.

Would Creed survive such a horrible accident? She tried to slow her breathing. He had to live. He *had* to.

On her way to the airport, by phone she tracked down the hospital that Creed would most likely be taken to, the one closest to the arena he'd been in tonight. She turned on a local sports station on the radio where the DJs were giving blow-by-blow accounts of the tragic ride.

Tears blurred her vision as she shut off the radio and she almost missed her exit to the airport. She had to get a grip and get herself together before she ended up in an accident.

Everything took too damn long from the time Creed had been hurt to the time she boarded the plane.

It was a direct flight but it still was interminably long. She almost forgot her carryon when it was time to get off the plane in the Albuquerque airport. She rented a car and used her phone's GPS to get herself to the hospital.

"Where is Creed McBride?" she asked in a rush when she reached the information desk in the ER.

The nurse checked the computer. "Only immediate family is allowed to see him."

"I'm his fiancé." She said the first thing that came to her mind.

The nurse looked at Danica for a moment then nodded. She gave Danica directions on how to get to Creed's room and she turned and rushed there.

When she reached the room there was a couple of men sitting outside. A wizened cowboy was sitting on a chair, his forearms resting on his thighs and his hat in his hands. The other cowboy was much younger and had his shoulder hitched up against a wall, his arms crossed over his chest.

"How is he?" she asked as she reached them. She could hear the panic in her voice.

"Nurse says he's in stable condition," the older man said in a deep Texan drawl.

"Won't let us go in the room and see him, though," said the younger cowboy.

A nurse came out of Creed's room and saw Danica. "Are you a family member?"

Danica nodded. "His fiancé."

The cowboys looked at her with interest, but she didn't care. She'd say whatever it took to see Creed, no matter who was there.

"How bad is he?" Danica asked.

"He has some broken ribs, a punctured lung, a broken arm, a concussion, and he's beat up pretty good." The nurse shook her head. "Crazy bull riders."

The nurse let Danica into the room and she slowly moved to

Creed's bedside. She sucked in her breath. His head was bandaged, as was his chest, and one of his arms was in a sling. He looked a bit pale as his gaze met hers. But then he gave a little smile.

"So you're talking to me again?" he said and winced like it hurt to talk. "What are you doing in New Mexico?"

Tears bit at the backs of her eyes. "I was so worried about you." She swallowed. "I watched it all on TV and caught the first plane to Albuquerque."

He studied her. "I'm glad to see you."

"I'm glad to see you, too." She shook her head. "But not like this."

"I never cheated on you, Danica." His gaze held hers.

She sank into the chair beside the bed. "Shhh. We can talk about that later."

"I want to get it cleared up now." He reached out his good arm toward her. She took his hand, which was warm and dry. "Teri is my cousin and I'm helping her through a rough time in her life."

Danica paused a moment, feeling off balance. "I saw a picture of you kissing her. Or at least that's what I thought it was."

"A picture?" Creed looked confused and then a little angry. "You had me followed?"

Danica shook her head. "Barry did. I knew nothing about it until he showed me photographs of you and the woman—Teri."

"Why didn't you give me a chance to explain?" he asked.

"The pictures are pretty damning." She sighed. "There were dated photographs with times of you two at dinner, and then you going into a hotel with her and coming out a couple of hours later." She took a deep breath. "It didn't look innocent."

Creed studied Danica. "Teri has been going through drug and

alcohol rehabilitation and her husband left her. My brothers and I are the only family she has left, and she and I are the closest out of all of us."

"I'm sorry." Danica looked at her hands before looking at Creed again. "I should have talked with you about it."

"I get it." He shifted in bed and grimaced. "I might have felt the same way."

She lowered her head before looking back at him. "I don't suppose you'll forgive me?"

"Forgive you?" He squeezed her hand. "Don't even worry your pretty little head about it. I'm just glad you're here and you understand now."

They held each other's gazes as she spoke. "I care so much for you that I can't even think straight about it."

"I know." He grinned. "Otherwise you wouldn't have told the nurse you're my fiancé."

Her face warmed. "It was the only way I could see you."

"You love me," he said with clear confidence.

Her jaw dropped. "I—"

"Admit it." He was still grinning. "You love me."

Her mind whirled. Was what she felt love for him? And even if it was true, was she ready to admit it to him?

"You're awfully arrogant and sure of yourself." Her face wasn't just warm now, it was burning.

"Yep." He squeezed her hand. She'd forgotten he was holding it.

She closed her eyes for a moment and took a deep breath.

When she opened her eyes she met his gaze. "Yes, damn it. I love you, Creed."

His expression changed to almost serious. "I fell for you the moment I saw you in that bar in Las Vegas. I watched you for a long time before I talked to you, and I knew that I had to make you mine. It's like I've loved you as long as I can remember."

The feelings whirling through her almost made her head spin. She was in love with Creed and he loved her.

He tugged on her hand. "Now come here and kiss me."

She rose up from the chair and leaned over him. "I don't want to hurt you."

"My lips are the only thing that don't hurt right now," he said with a laugh.

She smiled and leaned down to kiss him. It was a soft, sweet kiss, and she felt his love flowing into her. She hoped that he could feel hers as it poured out of her.

When she drew back, he was smiling. "When I get out of here, I'm going to show you just how much I love you."

She raised an eyebrow. "I don't think you're going to be doing much of anything for a while."

"Then you don't know me very well," he said in a teasing voice.

She groaned. "There's no keeping you down."

"Nope." He gripped her hand and drew her closer. "Now kiss me again."

CHAPTER 19

Danica decided to take the bull by the horns—so to speak. It was Sunday and she'd just returned from New Mexico and she found herself on Barry's doorstep, a manila envelope in her hand.

She pressed the doorbell and when there wasn't an answer she pressed it again. Barry's muffled but irritated voice came from the other side of the door. *"I'm coming."*

He jerked open the door and surprise registered on his face then pleasure. "Come in." He stepped aside and she walked into his home. His home was elegant and beautiful. It was a home meant to show off his wealth and status—whatever that was.

When she faced him, his smile faded when he got a good look at her expression.

"What's wrong?" He frowned. "Did that cowboy do something else to you?"

Danica raised the envelope, turned it upside down, and pieces of the photographs that he'd given her floated down. She'd put the photographs through her shredder and now they were scattered across his carpet.

"What the hell?" He raised his hands. "What are you doing?"

"These are the pictures you gave me." She tossed the envelope onto the floor. "That was his cousin. He's been helping her out."

Barry sneered. "What an interesting relationship he has with his cousin."

Anger that had been burning beneath the surface of her skin rose up inside her. She raised her hand and slapped him.

His head snapped to the side. His expression was one of surprise as he brought his hand to his cheek.

"I've had it, Barry. You stay away from me and you stay out of my life." She pointed her finger at him. "I'm in love with Creed and I intend to marry him." It didn't matter that he hadn't actually asked her, but Barry didn't need to know that.

He looked at her in shock. "Danica—"

"No." She shook her head. "You don't get to talk. You listen."

His mouth snapped shut.

"You come near me again and I'll file a restraining order against you." She stepped into his space. "I've tried to be nice, I've tried to remain friends. Obviously that hasn't worked. So now just stay the hell away from me."

His face flushed red. "When he screws you over, don't come running to me."

"You are the last person on earth that I would *ever* go running to about anything." She tilted her chin and clenched her fists at her sides. "Good bye, Barry."

She strode to the door, flung it open, and then slammed it shut behind her.

The anger that had been bubbling up inside her seemed to evaporate and float off in the breeze. That chapter in her life had finally come to a full close.

CHAPTER 20

Music throbbed in the air and the roar of the crowd filled the arena. Danica's stomach turned as it always did when Creed competed.

Three months following Creed's accident—"wreck"—with the bull, Danica and her entire family, along with Creed's brothers and his cousin, Teri, were there. It made for sixteen of them having made it to Las Vegas for the bull riding world championship. Creed had remained in the lead for the world title, but needed a win tonight to secure the championship.

Creed had gone back to riding six weeks after his injuries, which had worried Danica to no end. Maybe she *was* a worrier—at least when it came to Creed.

She rubbed her arms with both hands to try and alleviate her nervousness. She was in the middle of their family mob.

The last three months had been up and down. It had been so difficult being away from Creed and only seeing him sporadically. They spent all the time they could together, but it wasn't enough as far as either one of them was concerned.

Kelsey was doing much better and Darryl was still in jail. Danica had told Creed about what had happened and he'd been upset with her for talking to Darryl alone, concerned that Darryl could have hurt her, too.

Of course Darryl being in jail for battery had knocked him out of the running for the bull riding championship.

A hard knot lodged in Danica's chest as she looked at the mammoth screen that announced Creed would be riding The Machine again. The same bull that had trampled him three months ago and put him into the hospital.

She clenched her hands into fists and bit her lower lip. This was crazy. What if it happened all over again?

"I don't know how much more of this I can take." Danica sucked in her breath and let it out in a slow exhale. "Always wondering if the bull is going to get the better of him again."

"I bet it's hard," Carly said from beside Danica. "I can't imagine how I would feel if Dillon put his life in danger all of the time." She glanced at her husband who sat on the other side of her. "I might have to kill him myself."

A smile twitched at the corner of Dillon's mouth. "And I was thinking about taking up bull riding, too."

Carly slapped him on the shoulder. "Don't even think about it."

He laughed and Danica shook her head.

She looked back at the chute and saw Creed was now settling on the back of The Machine. The bull thrashed as much as it could in the narrow chute, knocking Creed around. When the bull had settled a little, Creed secured the bull rope around his hand, preparing for his ride.

Danica found herself holding her breath as Creed gave the signal that he was ready.

The gate swung open and The Machine flung itself into the arena. It twisted and bucked as if it was bent on dislodging its rider then killing him.

But this time, Creed rode him like he was on smooth water. His body fell into the rhythm of the ride and he matched every move the bull made.

Danica stood, her hands clasped, as the clock ticked each agonizing second down. When the horn sounded out at eight seconds, the crowd roared. Danica didn't. She was too worried now about Creed getting *off* the bull. That was where things had gone terribly wrong the night the bull could have killed him.

Creed hopped off The Machine, landed on his feet, and jogged several feet away. The bullfighters kept the bull's attention and Creed took off his hat and waved it at the crowd. He looked directly at Danica and she knew his smile was just for her.

"Ninety-five point five is Creed McBride's score!" shouted one of the announcers. "The top score of the night by three points."

Danica sat down in her seat and let her breath out in a huff. That was it. The end of the season and a reprieve from worrying about him for a while.

"Creed McBride has a special message for a special lady," the announcer said.

The crowd started cheering and Danica's gaze shot to the huge screen.

Danica, will you marry me?

Her heart started pounding and she held her hand to her chest as she stared at it. Her family and Creed's cheered as they shouted to Danica words of congratulations.

A buzzing started in her ears and she almost couldn't hear the announcer say, "Come on down, little lady."

She felt like she was in a daydream as she made her way down the aisle, past family members patting her on the shoulder and the back.

The crowd chanted "*yes, yes, yes…*" as she made her way down to the arena.

She was helped through a gate and when she was at the top of the steps, Creed caught her by her waist, swung her down. She nearly lost her breath as he set her on the ground. He took her by the hand and led her to where an announcer was holding a microphone.

When they reached him, Creed got down on one knee and took a ring from the ring box that one of the bullfighters was holding for him.

Danica found herself shaking, her heart pounding like crazy. Creed was asking her to marry him in front of thousands and thousands of fans and who knew how many were watching on television.

Creed held up the ring. "Will you marry me, Danica?" His words went over the loudspeakers as the announcer held the mic close to him.

Danica found her voice as she looked into Creed's hopeful

gaze.

"Yes," she said and her voice reverberated through the arena. "I will marry you."

The crowd exploded with applause as Creed grinned and slipped the huge diamond ring on her finger.

He picked her up and whirled her around and she hung on with her arms clasped around his neck.

"All of those buckle bunnies out there now know that you're off limits," she said with a grin, her voice coming out over the loud-speakers.

"Damn straight," Creed said and then kissed her hard enough to make her head feel like it was spinning.

When she drew back she smiled at him. "I love you, Creed McBride."

He set his western hat on her head. "You've got my love, honey. Always and forever."

* * * * *

After Creed was awarded his World Champion belt buckle, they took the next flight to Arizona and then drove to Prescott where Creed said he had a surprise for her.

As if being proposed to in front of the world wasn't surprise enough.

The flight had seemed a little surreal. She couldn't believe she was marrying Creed. Before he proposed, they hadn't even discussed where they would live, their occupations, or anything else.

But that didn't matter—they'd work things out. What she really cared about was Creed and spending the rest of her life with him.

After they arrived at Sky Harbor Airport in Phoenix, they picked up his truck from long term parking and headed off into the night. Once they were on their way to Prescott, Creed reached over and squeezed her hand where it rested on the console.

"We have a lot to talk about," he said as he glanced from the road to her and then back to the road.

"Yes, lots." She nodded.

"There are things I want to keep a surprise." His gaze met hers again. "Do you mind waiting?"

She gave a happy sigh. "I think I'm starting to love surprises."

On the ride to Prescott, every time she'd bring up something related to their future together, he'd shake his head and grin. Maybe she wasn't so crazy about surprises after all.

They were just outside of town when Creed made a quick call, saying they would be arriving soon. He wouldn't tell her who he had called.

When they arrived, he drove them straight to the B & B and she smiled at him with delight. Lights glowed in the windows and the moon was bright. Creed checked them in and she was excited to find that they had the same room that she had stayed in before… The room where she'd almost succumbed to temptation.

He let her go in first.

Danica caught her breath in yet another moment of surprise.

Every surface was covered with flickering red candles in glass hurricane lamps, and vases of red roses. Rose petals and a single long-stemmed rose lay across the king-sized bed and there was a trail of rose petals that led into the bathroom. Candlelight sparkled on the glass vases and hurricanes, and was reflected in the mirrors of the darkened room. The room was filled with the perfume of fresh cut roses.

"This is amazing." She turned to face Creed and flung her arms around his neck. "Thank you for the surprise. I love it." She glanced at the room then back at him with a smile. "Red roses are my favorite, too."

"That's what your brothers told me." He smiled down at her.

She raised an eyebrow. "You let my brothers in on this?"

"Not everything." He caught her left hand and raised it up and her diamond ring glittered in the room's dim light. "I'm amazed and floored by your beauty inside and out every single time we're together."

She'd never seen such a romantic side to him and it made her heart squeeze.

His mouth met hers in a sweet, loving kiss, a kiss that grew into something deeper and more passionate.

He led her to the bed and pushed aside some of the roses and had her sit on the edge of the mattress. He pulled off her boots, followed by her socks, then took off his own. He set his Stetson on a chair.

When they were both in their bare feet, he drew her up to stand and slid his fingers through her hair. She reached for the buttons on his shirt and began undoing them. He kissed the corner of her mouth then straightened as she pushed his shirt from his shoulders and he let it fall from his arms to the floor.

In the flickering candlelight, shadows danced across his dark features. She ran her palms over the expanse of his muscular chest, feeling the smooth skin over taut muscle. He moved her hands aside and began unbuttoning her blouse. He let it fall open and traced his fingers along the contours of her black bra, stroking her soft skin.

He gently slipped her blouse down her arms and he set it aside on a chair before returning his attention back to her.

"I can't believe you're mine," he said as he unhooked her bra, baring her breasts, and set aside the bra. "To have such an amazing woman to call my own is more than I ever thought possible."

"I feel as though I'm in a dream." She pressed her naked breasts against his chest. "Don't let me wake up."

"It's no dream." He slid his hands between them, down her belly to the button of her jeans. He unfastened them then pulled down her zipper.

She gripped his biceps as he pushed down her jeans and black panties and she stepped out of them. When she was naked he kissed her again as he slowly stroked her curves, his palms following the contours of her soft body.

Next went his belt then his Wrangler jeans and boxer briefs and then they were both naked. He pressed his body to hers, his cock hard against her belly, and he kissed her again.

He stepped back and took her by her hand and they followed the trail of rose petals to the bathroom. The petals were soft beneath her feet.

More roses and candlelight filled the bathroom. Red petals led to the huge jetted tub. He turned on the water, running it until it was a warm temperature. A couple dozen rose petals were on the bottom and they floated to the surface as he ran the water. He added bubble bath and then they both stepped into the tub. As she sank into the bubbles and rose petals, he turned on the jets.

Shampoo and bathing gel, along with a scrubby were on one

corner. He shampooed her hair, his touch firm as he rubbed her scalp. As the jets massaged her body, he slowly washed her, paying close attention to her breasts and her inner thighs, teasing her with every movement he made.

When it was her turn, she soaped his hair and rinsed it with water from the faucet. She scrubbed his torso and when she moved the scrubby downward beneath the water, she found he had a huge erection and she smiled.

He drew her onto his lap and she dropped the scrubby into the bath water. His cock pressed against her folds as she brushed her breasts against his chest and kissed him.

It was a kiss filled with passion and meaning and everything she wanted him to know... Just how much she loved him and how happy she would be as his wife.

He picked up a foil packet that he'd set beside the shampoo and opened it. She adjusted herself on his legs so that he could sheathe his cock and then she rose up and slowly slid herself down on his cock. He always filled her so well and tonight she felt as if she'd never felt him so deep or so thick.

She began to ride him in a slow and steady rhythm. He placed his hands on her hips and gripped her as he rose up to meet her.

Her breathing became harsher as she felt him inside her and the jetted water against her skin. She tipped her head back and rode him harder and harder as a climax began building inside her, greater and greater and greater.

Scents of roses and bubble bath, the dancing candlelight, the feel of his skin against hers and his cock inside her, all combined together and whirled within her. Faster and faster it seemed to swirl until all of the sensory collided.

Her eyes widened as her orgasm burst inside her. She cried out as she came, her body rocking from the strength of her climax. He thrust harder in and out and then he came with a loud groan. His cock throbbed as her core spasmed.

As she slowly slipped back down to earth, he held her close, both of them breathing hard.

When they were both down from their orgasm highs, she rose up and kissed him then drew away and smiled.

"Thank you," she said. "For all of this."

"I would do anything for you." He brushed her wet hair over her shoulder in a gentle movement. "Anything."

They climbed out of the cooling water and he dried her off with a fluffy towel and then she dried him off in return. He took her by the hand and led her to the bedroom.

In the bedroom he picked up the single long-stemmed rose to her from off the bed and pulled back the comforter and sheet for them to slide under. He helped her onto the bed and arranged pillows behind her and then himself.

"You are amazing," she said with a smile.

"Just wait 'til you see my surprises," he said with a grin.

She raised an eyebrow. "More surprises?"

In response he leaned over and grabbed a big black duffel from beside the bed that he'd dropped there when they walked in. He brought out a binder and held it as he looked at her.

"We haven't talked about our future in regards to now, but I have some things to show you."

Intrigued she leaned against his shoulder and looked so see that there were eight by ten photos in the binder. The photographs were of a ranch house, a barn, corrals, and other buildings, along with livestock.

"This is a ranch I want to buy," he said. "For us. It's not far from here and I think you would love it."

Butterflies fluttered in her belly. He was asking her to leave everything to move here.

He continued to turn over the last photo and beneath that was a piece of letterhead and he handed it to her.

"There are two positions open at Northern Arizona University," he said. "I think you have a good chance if you're interested. You have the qualifications and it's similar work to what you do now in San Diego."

Her lips parted in surprise as she looked at him. Before she could say a word, he took her by the shoulders.

"If you want me to move to San Diego, I will," he said. "But if you're willing, and you would be happy, I'd love to settle here and start a family."

Tears started rolling down her cheeks, coming out of nowhere. She flung her arms around him and hugged him tight.

She leaned back and he brushed tears from her eyes with his thumb. "Let's get that ranch," she said.

He grinned. "Are you sure?"

She nodded and she knew her smile was brilliant. "I'm sure."

"I have a couple more bull riding seasons left in me before I retire." He grew quieter. "I can ride on weekends and come back during the week." He paused as he searched her gaze. "Can you live with that?"

"It won't be easy." She gave him a soft smile. "But I wouldn't have it any other way. I want you to be happy."

"Just being with you and having you as my wife…" He shook

his head. "I could never be any happier." He placed his forehead against hers. "Thank you for saying yes. I love you so much that I can barely think sometimes when we're together."

She drew back and looked into his eyes. "I can't imagine my life without you. Thank you for all the wonderful surprises and for thinking about me in so many ways." She touched his stubbled face, which had become so dear to her. "I love you, Creed."

He put his arm around her shoulders and held her close. She couldn't wait for tomorrow. Couldn't wait for the rest of their future together.

# # #

ALSO BY CHEYENNE MCCRAY

CHEYENNE WRITING AS JAYMIE HOLLAND

Excerpt... *Satin and Saddles*

Cheyenne McCray

Carly Abbot set aside her glass of champagne on a tray as her closest friend, now Sabrina Holliday Cameron, motioned for her to come closer.

"It's time for me to toss the bouquet." Sabrina's smile was brilliant as she spoke to Carly. "Maybe you'll catch it."

"You know I'm not the marrying kind." Carly shook her head but returned Sabrina's smile.

"Just come on." Sabrina waved Carly to join her outside in the resort hotel's courtyard, where the wedding had been held.

Carly looked at her friend, exasperated. "I really don't want to."

"For me. Please?"

"All right, all right." Carly smiled. "You don't have to beg or call in the best friend card."

Sabrina grinned. "I knew you'd do it for me."

Carly pushed her dark hair over her shoulders. She brushed her palms over her curvy figure, along the royal blue satin dress she'd worn as the maid of honor. She smoothed out the material before she followed Sabrina.

"Time for all the single ladies to gather close." Sabrina's mother, Tessa, lightly hit the side of her crystal champagne glass with her cake fork. "The beautiful bride is going to toss the bouquet now."

Sabrina's three sisters, along with several other women, joined each other as Sabrina turned her back with her bouquet in her hands.

Reluctantly, Carly stood in the middle of the crowd of women and waited as Sabrina raised the bouquet and tossed it over her shoulder.

The bright flowers sailed through the air and came down toward one of Sabrina's sisters. The pretty woman caught the edge of bouquet over her head, stopping it with her fingertips. But the bouquet's momentum was a little faster than she'd expected. She hampered the flowers' trajectory just enough that they dropped straight down on Carly.

Instinctively she caught the bouquet, without intending to. The next thing she knew everyone was laughing and congratulating her. She wanted to pass the flowers to someone else but it was too late. She groaned.

"Ha." Sabrina grinned as she went up to Carly. "It was meant to be."

"Pleeeeease." Carly held up the bouquet. "This should go to one of your sisters."

"Too late." With a laugh, Sabrina set her hand on her friend's forearm. "Don't mess with fate."

Carly rolled her eyes. "As if."

"I know you're dating Mike for fun." Sabrina glanced toward the handsome best man. "Maybe it's time you break it off with him and find someone who rocks your boat."

"You're forgetting that I already did rock the boat that day we went fishing on the lake, and that was with Mike." Carly grinned at the memory of nearly capsizing the little fishing boat with her and

Sabrina ending up in the water. "That was good enough for me."

Sabrina laughed, a curl falling into her eyes, escaping the upswept hairdo. She brushed it out of her face. "That doesn't count. You pitched us both into the lake."

Carly shrugged. "Just goes to show that rocking my boat isn't enough."

"Hold onto those flowers." Sabrina pointed to the bouquet. "They belong to you now."

The moment Sabrina went off to join her new husband, Wyatt Cameron, Carly slipped away, into the resort hotel and to the room where they kept their purses. She set the bouquet with her purse. She was *not* going to carry that thing around, as if she was shopping for the marrying kind of man.

When she walked out of the room she nearly ran into Dillon Cameron and he caught her by her shoulders. Flutters exploded in her belly as she looked into his brilliant Cameron blue eyes and felt the heat of his palms through the satin bridesmaid's dress.

His brown hair was a little tousled from the breeze outside where the wedding had been and where the reception was currently being held. She swallowed past the sudden dryness in her throat as she looked at the exquisite picture the cowboy made in his black western tux that he'd worn as one of Wyatt's ushers.

All night, even during the wedding, her gaze had been drawn to the man as if her eyes had a mind of their own. He'd caught her at it a couple of times. She hadn't had a chance to meet him, but she'd wanted to.

Dillon gave a slow, sexy smile. "Carly, right?"

She simply nodded, unused to being at a loss for words. Heck, she was never at a loss for words. Why now? He released her and that seemed to release her tongue, too. "You're Dillon, Wyatt's brother."

"Yep." He smiled. "You're seeing Wyatt's best man, Mike Sharpe."

She shrugged. "We like to have a little fun together."

A sexy light appeared in his eyes as if she'd just given him an invitation. "Will you be at the party tonight?"

He was talking about the party that the bride and groom's friends were having once the pair took off for their honeymoon.

"I'm going with Mike." She took a step back, feeling suddenly nervous. "I'd better get back to the reception. See you around, Dillon."

I'm sure we will." His slow drawl sent a thrill through her body.

Heart pounding for no apparent reason, she turned and walked back toward the reception, feeling the heat of his gaze on her back.

Damn, she was hot. Dillon watched Carly head away, his gaze on the way her blue dress hugged her ass. The dress reached mid-thigh and she had long, sexy legs that stirred his imagination in a number of ways.

He headed toward the men's room, his thoughts consumed with the way the dress had bared her shoulders and clung to her curvy figure. If he didn't get his mind elsewhere, he was going to be sporting a hard-on throughout the rest of the party.

He'd caught her looking at him a couple of times during the wedding and reception with her beautiful lavender eyes, but he hadn't had a chance to get away from toasts and wedding photos long enough to talk to her. He'd known she was dating Mike, but didn't know the state of their relationship. Hell, he still didn't. For all he knew, Mike was serious about her. If he were, Dillon would back right off. But if Mike wasn't serious…

Just when he reached door to the men's room, Mike walked out and into the hallway. "Hey, Dillon."

"Hi, Mike." Dillon gave a nod. Speak of the devil. "I hear you're going to the party with that cute thing, Carly."

"She's that all right." Mike grinned. "Cute and sexy as hell."

Dillon hooked his thumbs in his belt loops. "What's the story with you two?"

With a shrug, Mike said, "We're good friends. Why, you interested in her?"

"Might be," Dillon said. "If you're just friends, mind if I ask her out?"

"You like to play the field, Dillon." Mike frowned and put his hands in his back pockets. "I don't want to see her get hurt."

"The last thing I want to do is hurt Carly." Dillon's expression was serious.

"If Carly wants to date you then I'm not standing in your way." Mike studied Dillon. "But you mess around with her feelings and I'm going to have to kick your ass all over the state."

"I have a feeling that woman can hold her own real well." Dillon slapped Mike on his shoulder. "See you at the poker game."

* * * * *

Carly braced her hands on the back of Mike's chair as she watched the poker game with the Cameron men along a couple of their friends, including Mike. He was holding his own and it was down to him and Dillon who had the biggest pile of chips.

Throughout the game she'd had a hard time keeping her eyes off a Dillon and again he'd caught her at it. Like the other men, he'd taken off his western tux jacket leaving him in a shirt that was snug across his muscular chest and fit his broad shoulders just right. He had his shirtsleeves rolled up and she liked watching the way the muscles in his arms flexed when he dealt. Every now and then their gazes would meet and she'd feel a warm flush throughout her body.

She looked over Mike's shoulder. He had a straight flush. He set his cards down and shoved most of his chips into the middle of the table.

Dillon studied Mike for a moment, then his cards. "I'm all in," he said and pushed everything he had in.

Mike looked at the remainder of his chips then looked at Dillon.

"Have anything else you'd like to wager?" Dillon asked.

Mike glanced up at Carly then back to Dillon. "Got anything in mind?"

Dillon met Carly's gaze. "The rest of the weekend with Carly if I win. If you win you can buy Rocket."

Carly's jaw dropped and the other men around the table hooted and laughed.

"That is one deal too good to miss," Ty Sharpe, Mike's cousin, said. "Mike's been trying to buy that stallion off Dillon for the past year."

"I think *not*," she said.

"Come on, Carly." Wayne, Dillon's brother, grinned. "You'll

sweeten the pot."

Zane nodded. "I'd like to see this."

Mike glanced up at Carly.

She put her hands on her hips. "Are you serious, Mike Sharpe? You'd trade me in a poker game?"

"Anything else you'd take?" Mike looked sheepish as he asked Dillon the question.

Dillon shook his head. "Carly or nothing."

Wayne laughed. "It's all in good fun, Carly."

She held back a smile. It was kind of funny—she'd never had men fight over her before—so to speak.

"Let me see your cards again, Mike." She sat on his knee and looked at his cards. A straight flush, ace to five. "All right." She glanced up at Dillon. "Do I have to sit in the middle of the table?"

The men chuckled.

"You're fine right where you are." Dillon leaned forward. "But when I win you have to come sit on *my* knee."

Carly felt her cheeks flush. She tilted her chin up. "Daytime only if you win. But when you lose, Mike gets to buy that horse."

"It's a deal." Dillon winked at her.

Mike laid down his cards. "Straight flush."

Dillon's eyes were totally on Carly as he laid down his own cards. "Royal flush."

Carly's eyes widened and this time she burned with heat all over. She had just been won in a poker game.

The men around the table were grinning and laughing. She tore her gaze from Dillon to Mike.

Mike wore a smile. "You know Dillon was just kidding."

Dillon shook his head. "I wasn't kidding.

She swallowed and met Dillon's blue eyes again. He patted his knee and beckoned to her.

"You can't be serious," Mike said. "That was a joke."

"Like I said, I wasn't kidding." Dillon looked at Carly. "You know I wasn't."

"You're right.." She stood. "When you made the bet I knew you were serious." She looked at Mike. "I guess I'm Dillon's for tomorrow."

"The deal was for the rest of the weekend," Dillon said.

Saturday and Sunday. She took a deep breath and walked over to him, hoping she wasn't blushing all over, and perched on his knee. He eased his arm around her waist and her whole body started tingling. Like earlier when she'd first talked to Dillon, she was at a loss for words at the moment, which was entirely unlike her.

She hadn't been this close to him before and she hadn't realized just how good he smelled. Of man and leather, a combination she loved.

Dillon stood, easing Carly to the floor and taking by the hand. "Time to cash out and head home." He looked at her. "How did you get here?"

"Mike." She glanced at Mike who had a bemused expression then she looked at Dillon. "He picked me up at my house."

Dillon slid his fingers over the back of her waist. "I'll get you home tonight and then in the morning, you're mine."

# # #

Excerpt... *Champagne and Chaps*

Cheyenne McCray

Wyatt Cameron's gaze slowly traveled the room as he leaned up against the bar, one elbow and forearm on the polished hardwood surface. The lights were low, the wood-bladed fans stirring the air that carried smells of bar food and beer.

Stampede Bar was warm from all of the bodies packed into it and filled with music, laughter, and chatter. Wyatt tapped one boot in time with the song the live band, El Rio, was playing. Cowboys and cowgirls danced a lively two-step on the sawdust-strewn dance floor.

A pair of pool tables took up one end of the massive room and it looked like some serious games were going on while a couple of cowboys were throwing darts at a dartboard at the other end of the room. Most of the high tops were filled and every stool at the bar was taken.

"See anything you like?" Mike Sharpe said over the fiddle playing.

Wyatt gave his buddy a quick grin then took another drink of his longneck beer. "Still looking," he said after a swallow. "I'll know her when I see her."

"Damn." Mike glanced toward the door and gave a low whistle. "Take a look at that tall, sexy drink of water."

Wyatt turned his attention to the door. His gaze went straight past the curvy woman to the petite gal behind her and his gut tightened. Light brown hair with blonde streaks, big eyes, and the type of smile that lit up even the dim bar. She was so damned pretty that he couldn't take his eyes off her.

Wyatt said as he studied the woman who'd caught his eye, "I think I just fell in love with that little thing next to her."

Mike looked amused. "Why don't you turn on that Cameron charm and go meet the lady?"

Wyatt considered it for a moment. He didn't want to pounce the moment they walked in the door. Well, maybe he did, but it wasn't the real smart thing to do. "I'll give them a moment to settle in."

He watched the two as they made their way to the only available high top in the room. The petite woman wore a red blouse and blue jeans that hugged her cute little ass. A silver chain with a small medallion was at her throat and small silver hoops on her ears.

He couldn't get himself to look away. She must have felt his gaze on her because she looked up and gave him a little smile before turning back to her friend.

"If that isn't your cue, I don't know what is," Mike was saying. "I think you'd better get your ass over there before someone beats you to it."

Wyatt grinned to himself. Damn, that woman was cute as hell. "I think you're right."

He set his empty longneck on the bar and headed toward the woman he had to have.

"That cowboy you just smiled at is on his way over." Carly's startling lavender eyes met Sabrina's gaze. "I knew you'd be flirting from the moment you walked in."

"I was not flirting." Sabrina's heart beat a little faster. "And you know I'm not ready to meet any guys."

Carly combed her fingers through her dark hair. "You're plenty ready. It's been seven months since you and the idiot broke up."

Idiot was right. Stephen was definitely one of those not-so-rare breeds.

Sabrina shook her head. "That's not all. You know what I mean."

"No, I don't know," Carly said. "There's no reason you can't get out and start living now."

Sabrina held one palm to her belly. "I don't know. I think it's too soon—"

"That is one incredibly fine cowboy," Carly interrupted. "Fine, fine, fine."

That was so true, Sabrina thought as she watched the man's easy approach from the corner of her eye.

He was tall and had a cowboy's build with broad shoulders and lean hips. He wore a white dress shirt and a white Stetson along with Wrangler jeans. The shirt in no way disguised his muscular chest and arms.

Yummy.

Sabrina's stomach flipped as the cowboy held her gaze and walked up to their table. He touched the brim of his hat as he looked from Sabrina to Carly.

"I'm Wyatt Cameron," he said with a sexy smile that made her stomach drop to her toes.

Carly extended her hand. "Carly Abbot."

Sabrina jumped when Carly elbowed her. Sabrina cleared her throat and offered her own hand. "Sabrina Holliday."

His touch was warm as he gripped her hand for a few moments and held her gaze. A shiver ran down her spine as she met his gorgeous brilliant blue eyes.

"Are you part of the Cameron crew that I hear so much about over in the San Rafael Valley?" Carly tilted her head to the side. "You have a bunch of brothers."

"That would be me." Wyatt had a spark of amusement in his eyes as he released Sabrina's hand. "Three brothers and a sister."

Carly smiled. "I figured."

"Mind if my friend and I sit with you?" Wyatt nodded in the direction of another good-looking cowboy who was leaning up against the bar.

"We don't mind at all," Carly said.

Sabrina felt mute. Wyatt Cameron had all the makings of a man she could really enjoy being around. But she didn't want that… Didn't want to get close to any man. She was all for Carly's determination that tonight was all about flirting and fun.

Wyatt took a seat at the high top and gave a signal to the other cowboy who started coming their way. When the cowboy arrived, Wyatt made introductions.

"Mike, this is Sabrina and Carly." He gestured to each of them. "Sabrina and Carly, this is Mike Sharpe who's also from the valley."

"A pleasure." Mike smiled and shook each of their hands.

Carly gave a slow nod. "I think I've heard of your family, too," she said to Mike. "You own Sharpe Feed and Tack in Patagonia?"

"My cousin, Ty Sharpe, owns the feed store," Mike said. "I have a ranch on the other side of Wyatt's."

"The Sharpe family owns this bar, too, don't they?" Carly asked. "A friend mentioned it the last time I was here."

"That would be another cousin who owns Stampede." Mike glanced around the room. "Brady's probably around here somewhere."

"Where are you ladies from?" Wyatt's gaze settled on Sabrina.

Her cheeks warmed at the intense look of interest in his eyes. "Tucson."

"What part of town?" he asked.

She cleared her throat. "The foothills."

His gaze slid to Carly. "Whereabouts are you? Tucson, too?"

Carly shook her head. "Patagonia." She glanced at Sabrina. "Sabrina is staying with me for the summer."

Sabrina wanted to kick Carly under the table but she was afraid she would kick one of the men. She really didn't want these cowboys to know she'd be a lot closer to them than Tucson. This Wyatt might think she'd be interested in seeing him more, and all she wanted was a little fun.

But then again, she might be thinking too much into this. She'd barely met the guy. Still, she really didn't want to seem accessible to anyone. That was part of the reason why she'd let Carly talk her into staying for the summer. She needed time alone.

Wyatt's smile made Sabrina's toes curls. Damn, he was hot.

"Dance?" he asked and gestured to the floor as a new tune started.

Carly was busy chatting with Mike when Sabrina looked over at her friend.

I should just let loose just like we planned, Sabrina thought. She missed her old self. There was a time when she would have been flirting like Carly and just having fun without worrying about the possibility that the guy would want to get into a relationship. She needed that again. She needed to let her hair down and just have fun.

With a smile she looked back at Wyatt. "Sure."

He surprised her by helping her down from the tall stool at the high top, then took her hand and led her to the dance floor.

Butterflies batted around in Sabrina's belly as they made it onto the floor, and he brought her close and they started to two-step. "I'm not very good at this." She raised her voice over the loud music as she stepped on Wyatt's boot. "To me two-stepping means one step on the floor and one on your boot."

"You're doing fine." He met her gaze, a glint of humor in his eyes. "Just don't run off is all I ask. I'd like to get to know you."

She didn't answer. She didn't plan on letting any man get to know her well. But it wouldn't hurt to have a little fun dancing with a cowboy. This was all about a fun night out.

"I'll think about it," she said with an answering smile.

By the time three songs had passed, Sabrina was laughing and enjoying herself more than she'd expected. Her skin was covered in a light film of perspiration and her heart was beating a little faster from the fast-paced tunes that they'd danced to.

She'd been having so much fun that she forgotten all about Carly. When she glanced back at the table, her friend was gone. She searched the dance floor with her gaze and smiled when she saw her friend talking with Mike to one side of the room.

Carly looked like she was having fun flirting with the cowboy, which was no surprise. If Carly was anything when it came to men, she was a flirt and a heartbreaker. Poor Mike, Sabrina thought and mentally shook her head. *You're in for some heartache if you're not careful.* Unless Carly actually considered settling for one man.

Ha. That'll be the day. Not after Carly's breakup. Ever since then she'd decided to flirt and play and that was good enough for her.

Sabrina caught her breath as Wyatt brought her into his embrace, catching her off guard. For a moment she wondered what he was doing and then realized the band had struck up a slow tune.

He drew her close and she felt his belt buckle dig into her belly and smelled the clean scent of his aftershave. Her stomach flip-flopped again as she felt a moment of panic. This was close, far too close to be allowing herself to get to a man.

But it felt so good being in his arms. She rested her palms on his shoulders and could feel the power in his body as they slowly moved on the dance floor. About six-three, he was almost a foot taller than she was and she felt more than petite in his arms. She breathed in his warm, masculine scent as they danced and found herself sighing. She loved the scent of a man.

# # #

Excerpt... *Lace and Lassos*

Cheyenne McCray

The next thing Kaitlyn knew, she was in his arms. "And I love having you in my home." Wayne's voice was low, deep, and thrills rolled through her.

A part of her said she should turn and run. That this was too much, too soon. But another part of her wanted what he could give her. What they could share.

She closed her eyes and let him hold her close, their bodies snug together. She breathed in his scent, letting it fill her completely.

When she opened her eyes, her gaze met his. She slid her arms around his neck and pulled him closer until their lips met and she kissed him.

The kiss was more powerful than the one he had given her at the party. This one was filled with years of longing and need so intense that she didn't know if she'd ever catch her breath.

She slid her hands into his hair, loving the soft strands slipping through her fingers and the feel of his scalp beneath her fingertips. She moved her hands down his neck and over his shoulders that were hard and muscular beneath her palms.

He kept her pressed up against him and she felt his erection against her belly. She ached between her thighs and she suddenly wanted her clothes off and to strip his away. She wanted to feel the heat of his naked skin against hers.

Their relationship had always been so sexually charged once they started having a physical relationship. They had matched each other in the depths of their desire and sexuality. She'd never felt anything with any man like she had with him. Not that her sexual experiences were extensive. She'd had all of three including Wayne and her ex.

Wayne kissed her even harder and she made soft sounds of want and need as she moved her hands down and explored his chest with her palms. He had held her by her waist but was now gripping her ass, pulling her impossibly closer to him. He raised her up and she wrapped her thighs around his hips and moved her arms around his neck again and he was carrying her to the bed.

The comforter was soft against her back and the mattress dipped beneath their combined weight as he rolled her onto her side so that they were facing each other. He kissed her then moved his lips to the corner of her mouth then moved them to her ear where he nipped her earlobe. She gasped with pleasure as it sent tingles through her body.

A part of her held back. She shouldn't be here, shouldn't be doing this. Not with all that was going on in her life… Not with all that had gone on.

But another part of her needed this. Needed to feel alive again. Needed to feel closeness to another person that she hadn't experienced for a long, long time.

She let everything slip away and let herself fall into being with Wayne. Being with him completely for the night where she wouldn't think of the past.

Not for tonight.

# # #

Excerpt... *Silk and Spurs*

Cheyenne McCray

Wind tugged at Jessie Porter's dark red hair as she climbed out of her red Mustang and her athletic shoes met Bar C ground. She pushed errant strands out of her face as she slowly looked around her at the Cameron family ranch. From what she knew of the place, it had been in the same family for generations.

A massive barn, extensive corrals, an old bunkhouse, and a sprawling ranch home edged the huge driveway. The parking area was big enough to accommodate a semi if need be, with enough room for the big rig to turn around. Everything was big on this ranch from what she could see.

The bawl of cattle in the distance told her that a herd was close. Lacy clouds were scattered across a blue early morning sky as the sun rose.

She reached into the passenger seat of her car and grabbed her backpack with her camera equipment, then slung it over her shoulder before pulling out her Nikon and looping the strap around her neck. The car door gave a solid thump as she slammed it shut and then she walked to the back of the vehicle. A big white work truck was parked on one side of her Mustang, on the other a sleek new black Ford crew-cab.

Gravel crunched beneath her shoes as she stepped away from the vehicles and raised her camera, looked through the lens, and started shooting.

More than likely the ranch's owner, Zane Cameron, would be out working but she wasn't sure where. She was bound to run into someone who did know as she began photographing the ranch. Too bad Danica, the youngest Cameron, wasn't going to be around. Danica had mentioned that she had to spend a week in New Mexico visiting a friend, so she wouldn't be here while Jessie was.

For cowboys, the days started before a rooster crowed. Jessie had intended to be at the Bar C when its cowboys climbed out of bed, but she'd overslept, forgetting to set her alarm and she hadn't started her drive from Tucson on time.

In this part of Arizona, the elevation was almost five thousand feet and the late October air was chilly in the mornings. The mornings warmed quick under the southern Arizona sun, so quick that at ten-thirty she was ready to remove her sweater, and the sun warmed her bare arms. Thanks to her sister's visit and subsequent amazing cooking, Jessie's jean shorts were feeling a little too tight this morning. She'd miss Tanya now that she was heading back to Houston, but her waistline just might recover.

She focused her lens on the ranch house that was built of dark wood. From the front it looked like it was well over four thousand square feet, but who knew what it actually was—it could be much larger. She'd heard that the Camerons had done well for themselves, and by the looks of it, that was true. Between the four brothers and their respective ranches, they had a virtual empire in the San Rafael Valley.

It was only recently that she'd become friends with Danica, the youngest sibling in the family. She was the reason Jessie had been hired to photograph the ranch, and soon the impending wedding of Zane, the eldest son.

Tall, stately old sycamore trees, mesquites and a few native oaks shaded the house. An enclosed porch ran the length of the home and through the screen she saw a variety of plants hanging from the rafters. More potted greenery was arranged around chairs and beside the loveseat-sized white porch swing. A rooster weather vane perched on one end of the rooftop that she captured with its luscious blue-sky background.

Colorful flowerbeds had been planted in front of the house— pansies, chrysanthemums, and carnations were beneath the Arizona October sun.

An old wooden wagon wheel leaned up against an oak that had an old fashioned triangular dinner bell hanging from it. It made for an excellent photo. To the left of the home was a well-shaded area with a covered swing, and she heard the sound of a small waterfall as it trickled into a pond.

Behind the house rose a tree line along with a weathered windmill that made rusted scraping sounds as the blades turned with the wind. She wondered if the windmill actually pumped water for the house or if it was unused and simply remained from decades gone by. She'd head out back and photograph it, too.

Colorful birds darted in and out of the trees, chirping and shrieking, and she saw a lizard scale a wall of the house.

She captured everything with a practiced eye and knew the photographs were going to turn into one fabulous collection when she was done. This place was a photographer's dream. From what little she'd seen, she had the feeling that she could spend hours here and still not catch everything that she wanted to.

"Can I help you?"

A deep, masculine drawl from behind her send a shiver down her spine and she lowered her camera and let it hang around her neck. She turned to face one hell of a fine cowboy, easily one of the sexiest she'd seen in all of her twenty-nine years.

At least six-three with broad shoulders and a cowboy's build, he had blue flame eyes and black hair that curled slightly beneath his cowboy hat. His skin was well tanned and his arms roped with muscle.

"Sure." She smiled. "You can help me anytime." He raised an eyebrow and she grinned as she held out her hand. "Jessica Porter," she said. "But please call me Jessie. I'm here to photograph the ranch and the upcoming wedding."

"You're my kid sister's friend." The cowboy took her hand in a firm grip. "Welcome to the Bar C."

Jessie's heart started to pound like crazy as the cowboy's warm touch sent fire through her body. Her mouth grew dry and she bit the inside of her lower lip. It was the most enticing reaction that she'd ever had to a man.

Before he released it, he said, "I'm Zane Cameron."

The disappointment that swept through her was a surprise. She didn't even know Zane, so what difference did it make that he was getting married in just weeks?

What a shame. All of that hot man flesh would soon belong to some other woman.

The green-eyed redhead was so sexy that he'd damned near gone hard when he'd clasped her hand. She had a cute grin and shapely body and her nipples were hard, poking against the light cotton of her T-shirt.

She wasn't wearing a bra.

For one moment Zane thought about carting Jessie off to the ranch house and taking her six ways 'til Sunday.

Well hell. He mentally shook his head. He had no business thinking about another woman and his body had no damned excuse to react the way it had.

Except that Jessie Porter was one hell of a woman. And he was a red-blooded American male and he'd just had a natural reaction to her.

Keep telling yourself that, Cameron.

"Congratulations," she said. Her smile was enough to make him crazy.

For a moment he didn't know why she was telling him congratulations, but then he regained his senses.

"Thanks." He hooked his thumbs in his belt loops, feeling like he needed to anchor them to make sure he kept his hands off of her.

She tilted her head to the side, which caused her dark red hair to slide away from her elegant neck. "Is the bride-to-be here?"

"Phoebe's at her place." He dragged his hand down his face then gave a nod in the direction of the house. "You can photograph anything you'd like to around here. Danica wants to give the album to our aunt."

Jessie nodded. "Danica mentioned that your aunt took care of the two of you along with your three brothers. Raising five kids is quite a feat for one woman."

"Sure as hell was." He glanced at Jessie as she fell into step beside him.

"Danica said two of your brothers are twins," she said. "Wayne and Wyatt."

Zane nodded. "Yep, and our youngest brother is Dillon."

Her smile was pure sunshine as she looked at him.

God only knew why he found himself comparing Phoebe with Jessie.

He'd begun to feel a little uneasy about his relationship with Phoebe and he'd managed to put off the wedding another couple of months, but here it was, creeping back up. To him Phoebe had been the picture of sweetness and intelligence, but lately it seemed that there had to be another side of her that others had seen but he hadn't, but then maybe it was the pressure of the wedding. It did concern him, though.

Ah, hell. Maybe his concern was just a case of pre-wedding jitters. Although he had a good mind to move the date again.

He glanced at Jessie and thought how different she looked from Phoebe who was pale blonde and petite at five-one. Jessie, on the other hand, was no shorter than five-eight. Both women were beautiful as hell, just as different as sunrise from sunset.

He ground his teeth. He'd never been one to compare women, especially not now that he was about to be married. It was time he settled down and had a couple of kids to carry on the Cameron name. No one else in the family seemed to be inclined to head down that road. Someone had to do it.

"Phoebe would like you to photograph her place, too." He paused in front of the doors to the ranch house. "She's got a nice home, just north before you hit the hills and she wants the pictures to market it."

"So, she's selling it now that you're getting married?" Jessie took her camera in both hands. "Of course she'll be moving to the ranch, I assume."

"You assume right." Zane tried not to frown. "Phoebe is reluctant to sell her place and has decided to rent it." Considering how pricey the house was, he wasn't sure she'd be able to find anyone who could afford to rent it in these parts. He'd just have to convince her to put it up for sale. There was no need to hang on to another property.

Zane held the screen door open that let out onto the porch. Jessie hitched her pack with her camera equipment on her shoulder and her shoes made soft sounds on the wooden floor as she passed through the door and cool air touched her face.

"I love this. Everything about your place is fantastic." She raised her camera and glanced at him. "I can photograph anything?"

"Almost anything." The corner of his mouth turned up in a look that was sexy enough to make her stomach flip. "When in doubt, just ask."

She nodded. "Sure."

As she took a few shots of the expansive porch, taking in antique ironwork objects decorating the area as he let the screen door close. When she lowered her camera, he opened the huge door to the ranch house. She stepped through the doorway and entered the spacious home.

Inside everything was big and roomy with western décor and artwork, and high vaulted ceilings. The beautiful hardwood floor had area rugs covering parts of it. A coffee table made from a tree trunk was in front of a long leather L-shaped couch and another fabric couch with a western design, both of which faced an enormous entertainment center and big screen TV. Picture windows showed the incredible views from the front and back.

Through an archway was a spacious kitchen that she wanted to get a better look at. From what she could see of it, she knew her sister the cook would love it.

Jessie had just started photographing the living room when a cell phone rang and she lowered her camera. She automatically put her hand to the phone she wore on a holster at her side but realized it was Zane's as she saw him take his phone from his own holster on his belt and he answer it.

His expression hardened as he listened to the caller. "I'll take care of it," Zane said and pressed the off button before re-holstering his phone. He looked at Jessie. "I need to leave to deal with a couple of hunters trespassing on my land."

"Can I go with you?" She let her camera hang from its strap around her neck and hitched the backpack up on her shoulder. "I'd love an opportunity to get a look at some of the scenery."

He paused for a moment then gave a nod. "Come on."

This time his stride was long and she had to double her steps to keep up with him as they headed outside to the big black Ford truck she had parked next to.

She hurried to the passenger side but he was there before her. He opened the door and she stepped up on the running board then climbed inside before he shut the door behind her.

He got in on the driver's side and put the key in the ignition and started it. The truck roared to life and he backed up then headed over the cattle guard and under the sign with the Bar C Ranch's name and brand. His presence was so powerful that she found it hard not to be completely aware of him. She glanced at his profile and almost forgot that he was hands-off.

Damn.

As she studied him, his gaze met hers for a brief moment and she felt the power of some kind of connection between them. Her heart beat faster and she felt a tingling sensation all the way to her belly. A muscle ticked in his jaw before he moved his gaze back to the road.

She took a deep breath and tried to shake off the incredible attraction she had for Zane Cameron.

Once she turned her attention to the scenery, she was again impressed by the canopy of dark green oaks that contrasted against the expanse of golden grass. Here and there were pockets cottonwood trees and a few massive sycamores.

"This country is amazing," she said. "An outdoor photographer's dream."

"I grew up here and I never get tired of it." He glanced over at her as he drove. "Most visitors here, including Arizona natives from other parts of the state, can't believe they're in Arizona. Had a guy from Santa Barbara out here and he couldn't believe how much it looked like the area he was from."

"The expanse of grass of the San Rafael Valley and the surrounding green hills is just beautiful," she said.

"Most people are surprised to learn that the musical *Oklahoma* was filmed right here in the valley," he said.

"I never would have guessed that." She raised her brows. "Parts of the grass valley look like how I would picture the Midwest plains back in the day."

She was in love with the country. So peaceful, so quiet, so stunning.

It wasn't long before they paused in front of a barbed wire fence with an open gate and a cattle guard. She looked at Zane.

"The 'No Hunting' signs have been taken down." He shook his head. "I'll have to get one of the men out here to take care of it."

Zane drove on and they came up on an old red truck parked in the shade of a group of tall oaks but no one was in sight. Up ahead was a stock tank and water tower.

She glanced at Zane again to see him frowning. He parked then opened his truck door and climbed out. She hurried out her side, her camera strap securely around her neck and she hopped onto the dry ground.

As soon as she was out of the truck she took in their surroundings, picking out what she felt would be the best shots in the beautiful scenery. She took a deep breath of the clean air and let it fill her entire being as she closed her eyes. She let all tension leave her body as she connected with the land.

"It's wonderful here." She opened her eyes and looked at Zane who was staring in one direction.

"Let's go this way. I can see some tracks leading up the road in this direction. We'll try and stay in the open and visible," he said as he looked over his shoulder at her. "The last thing you want is to get shot by mistake."

"Gotcha." She made sure she followed him and stayed out from behind the occasional oak tree or bush. "What's in season this time of year?"

"Whitetail called Coues deer." He paused and she almost ran into him as he gave a nod in the direction they had been walking. "Over there."

She peered past him and spotted two men, one wearing a cap,

and another in a brown cowboy hat, walking toward them.

A flash of irritation caused Zane's gut to burn. The men should have stopped by the ranch to ask permission to shoot on his land. It was the proper thing to do, but then the signs were down.

"How do you do?" one of the two men said as they met up and the man held out his hand. "I'm Bud Harper and this is Joe Cullman." Bud was tall, but Zane still had a good three inches on him. Joe was a little shorter and stockier.

"Zane Cameron." He took Bud's hand and shook it before taking Joe's and releasing it. "Did you know you're trespassing on private land?" Zane's tone kept his tone even, not showing any anger. "There's no hunting on this part of the ranch."

Joe pushed up his ball cap. "This your land?"

Bud glanced around. "We're sorry. We've been real careful to not trespass. We didn't see any signs."

"I own the Bar C." Zane gave a nod. "We're pretty welcoming to hunters, but we want to keep them out of this area of the ranch this year. Someone has taken down the signs and we'll be fixing that." He pointed toward the west. "If you take the dirt road another mile and a half, there's a sign that says Jones' Mesa. I've seen plenty of deer in that area and there are some great places to glass from and see a lot of country," he said. "Just do me a favor and go under the fences if you can rather than climb over them. Hunters damage a lot of fences. It's the only gripe I really have about you guys."

"Sure thing. We understand. We'll head on over there." Bud moved his gaze from the direction Zane had pointed to and looked at Zane again. "Much obliged."

Zane gave a nod and then Bud and Joe headed back to the beat-up red pickup, climbed in with Bud on the driver's side. The truck gave a rusted hiccup and then rumbled as Bud started it.

He noticed Jessie photographing the truck as the men left. She lowered her camera and looked at Zane. "You were pretty nice to those guys."

He rested his hand on the hood of his truck. "Nothin' wrong with a little hunting as long as it is in the right area and as long as they respect things."

"What does 'to glass from' mean?" she asked. "That's a term I've never heard before."

"Hunters use binoculars and spotting scopes to search the country for deer," Zane said. "It's called glassing. When they see deer through the binoculars, they stalk them."

"That's interesting," she said. "So what's next for a day in the life of a cowboy?" Her smile caused a stirring in his gut. "After chasing off hunters and all."

He studied her and it felt as if there was a war going on in his chest. "While we're out here I can give you a little more of a tour of the Bar C." Something about Jessie made him want to spend as much time as possible with her.

Not a good idea, Cameron. He mentally chided himself. *Run fast and run now.*

"Sure." She smiled. "I'd love that." She pointed in the direction of the fence line. "I saw a group of some kind of cool looking feathery looking plants over there that I'd like to photograph on the other side of the fence."

He gave a nod then watched her as she walked away from him. She had a cute little ass and gentle curves that were made for a man's hands to caress. And those long legs that weren't covered by her shorts. They were enough to make a man's mouth water.

Damn.

Jessie reached the barbed wire fence. He watched as she carefully grabbed a top strand between barbs and then did the same with her feet so that she was standing on the bottom strand and balancing as she took pictures.

Concerned that she might fall, he moved closer to her. Before he reached her, she lowered the camera and let it hang on the strap around her neck. She started to climb back down when he heard a ripping sound and then a curse.

He reached her and put his hand on her shoulder. "You okay?" he asked just as he looked down and saw that she'd shredded her T-shirt on the barbed wire.

His mouth went dry as he got a good look at her bare breast and the pert nipple. He swallowed and met her gaze.

Her cheeks had gone red hot and she held her T-shirt over her breast the best she could. "So much for this thing," she said, trying to make light of an embarrassing situation.

"We'll get you back to the house and you can wear one of my clean shirts." His touch set her on fire as he took her arm and she stepped down from the fence with his aid. "For now you can wear this one."

He released her then unbuttoned his shirt and slipped it off. Her jaw almost dropped as she got a good look at his tanned physique and the powerful play of muscles in his chest and arms.

If he wasn't about to be married she would have jumped him in two seconds flat.

"Thanks," she said as she took the shirt from him and smiled.

He helped her slip into the shirt as she fought to keep the scrap of cloth over her breast. His shirt had his scent, warm and masculine, and she found herself inhaling and savoring it.

Once the shirt was on, they walked back to his truck and he helped her into the cab. She kept her hand firmly over the tear as he shut the door behind her.

He climbed into the driver's seat and started the truck before glancing over at her. "Need a little help with that?" he said in a teasing voice.

"I think I've got it." Her cheeks had cooled but threatened to heat up again. "What happens on Cameron property stays on Cameron property, right?"

He laughed. "No problem."

# # #

ABOUT CHEYENNE

New York Times and *USA Today* bestselling author Cheyenne McCray's books have received multiple awards and nominations, including

RT Book Reviews magazine's Reviewer's Choice awards for Best Erotic Romance of the year and Best Paranormal Action Adventure of the year

*Three "RT Book Reviews" nominations, including Best Erotic Romance, Best Romantic Suspense, and Best Paranormal Action Adventure.

*Golden Quill award for Best Erotic Romance

*The Road to Romance's Reviewer's Choice Award

*Gold Star Award from Just Erotic Romance Reviews

*CAPA award from The Romance Studio

Cheyenne grew up on a ranch in southeastern Arizona. She has been writing ever since she can remember, back to her kindergarten days when she penned her first poem. She always knew one day she would write novels, hoping her readers would get lost in the worlds she created, just as she experienced when she read some of her favorite books.

Chey has three sons, two dogs, and is an Arizona native who loves the desert, the sunshine, and the beautiful sunsets. Visit Chey's website and get all of the latest info at CheyenneMc-Cray.com and meet up with her at Cheyenne McCray's Place on Facebook! Feel free to contact Chey at mailto:chey@cheyennemc-cray.com.

2809393R00114

Made in the USA
San Bernardino, CA
06 June 2013